MARTY & ME

Volume Two

JENNY'S JOURNAL

By

Mary Jean White

NOTES TO THE READER

This book is a work of fiction.
Names, characters, places or incidents
are either products of the author's imagination
or are used fictitiously.

The prices in the book reflect those
of 1961 to 1963,
when $1 would buy what
$8.40 to $8.60 in 2020 dollars would.

Second Edition

with major revisions
and added content

January 9th, 1963

Cher Marty,

I really miss you! Last Wednesday, it wasn't just at the airport that I made a fool of myself. When I got home, I started up again or rather went on crying. It was the middle of the night when I finally got to sleep. I was bummed out all weekend. Definitely not a fun person to be around!

Emalie rode to school with me and Mom and when I got to school Sunday evening, I started feeling better. It was good to see Sarah again (as well as having Emalie there too, of course).

I started up my therapy sessions with Dr. Jameson yesterday. She told me she attended a seminar with Albert Ellis last summer and picked up his new book, *Reason and Emotion in Psychotherapy*. It's about REBT. That's rational, emotive, behavioral therapy, but you know that, of course! She wants to use it in my therapy along with Carl Rogers's client-centered therapy. She explained (in layman's terms!) what those approaches were ('modalities' to you!).

Anyway, she wants me to write about what Dad did and things that have happened because of it. She said that lots of times, when bad things happen, you can start believing things that are just not true. Then, because of that thinking, you can start behaving in ways that are harmful to you, or at least that don't help you.

My therapy will be to change any unhealthy ways of thinking I have developed to healthy ones. She said doing that doesn't mean everything will magically get better. I'll always have hassles and problems I don't like, but I should change what I can, while accepting I won't be able change everything I don't like. What's important is to live the best way I possibly can.

I thought about using Dad's typewriter to type out the accounts of what happened, but I would feel weird being in his office even though he's still in Iran. (I need to talk to Dr. Jameson about that!).

So anyway, I decided I'm only going to work on it at school, using one of the typewriters available to students. I

1

think that's best. Also, I don't want Mom to see what I write by 'incident.'

About the regular paper I'm using. No more carbon paper! Though, I'm using a lot of 'Liquid Paper' to make corrections (Sigh!).

A graduate of Willard gave us a Xerox photographic copier! I don't know if you have one to use at the library at Southern, but wow! Now, if I make a mistake, I just have to change it on the original page. No more having to do it on the carbon copies too! Because, yeah! No carbon copies!

The woman who gave us the machine is a stock broker. We don't know her name because she gave it anonymously. There can't be a lot of women that are stock brokers though! Anyway, Sarah heard that it cost $2000! Can you believe it?

The copies aren't cheap when you compare it to the cost of carbon paper. (We pay $0.05 a copy). I hope you don't mind me spending the money. But it's so much easier than using carbon paper or having to type everything out twice! Or thrice! (very Brontë, that word!).

Anyway, about the 'accounts' for Dr. Jameson. I'm going to organize it like a journal with day by day accounts. I'm beginning on August 17th, 1961. Wow that's a year and a half ago! I can't believe it's been that long or all that's happened since then!

Okay, going ahead. Last summer I only told you about the 'incident' itself, but we didn't really discuss it that much, even when we met with Dr. Jameson. Now, though, I want to tell you all the stuff I remember about the whole week after Dad, well, abused me.

Dr. Jameson told me I should use the words 'abuse' if that was how I felt about it. She said it amounted to at least 'emotional abuse' in her viewpoint. I thank God it didn't turn into physical, sexual abuse! Like Karen thinks it did with Mike.

As I have been going over everything in my head, I have thought long and hard about what happened. I intend to even have Karen read what I write, as well as Dr. Jameson. Well, to see if Karen remembers it like I do. I also want Dr. Jameson to know how I felt (emotionally) about everything.

I do keep a diary, as you know, but I was so upset and so

much was going on, I didn't write about what happened at that time. So, I'm going to have to really think about everything and try to remember it like it happened. (That was an awful paragraph, but I don't feel like correcting it right now. I don't think I would do any better if I did).

Dr. Jameson said I should really take my time and think about not just the bad things, but see if I think of any good things that came out of the incident.

I guess there are some good things, like my friendships with Emalie and Sarah. Going to Willard is good too. Even though sometimes I get homesick and miss Mom and Karen (and I admit it, even Mike!). Willard is much better than even Hildreth and Hildreth is the best public school in Cambridge or even in the whole Boston area (in my opinion!).

I hope all my mistakes don't show up when I make the copies on the Xerox machine! (That's what they call the photographic copier). I'll send you a copy of what I write each week, so it will be spread out over all this winter, maybe even to March.

Should I mail it to you at home or care/of one of your students? I really don't want Aunt May to get her hands on it, but I'll do whatever you think best. Just let me know.

I'm not sure how many days I'm going to write about, but I'll start with 'that Thursday' and go through at least the next Wednesday when I took my entrance exams. But I may add more days. Like some things that happened later in the fall.

Next August, it will be great to see you at the reunion again. That seems like a long time off though! On that sad note, I say:

À bientôt! Avec tout mon amour,
Jenny

P.S. I reread this and I think I'm going to wait until you can give me the address of one of your students to mail it to. I don't want Aunt May to get her hands on it. So, I'm going to wait until after I talk to you to mail it.

P.P.S. I just realized these postscripts are useless, even stupid.

You won't get it until 'after' I talk to you. Like the 'time travel paradox' where someone travels back in time and kills your grandfather and keeps you from being born! I'm tired and thinking crazy (i.e. the P.S. and P.P.S. and adding another page to this letter!).

Ton amie idiote

Journal: Thursday, August 17th, 1961

It all happened at the end of the summer, just after we got back home from the family reunion. When we did, Grandmother McDonald was really sick and needed someone to take care of her pretty much full time.

She had a home nurse during the day, but Mom would go over the evenings to help her until the night nurse came. Grandmother's insurance didn't pay enough to cover a nurse 'round-the-clock', though, and she couldn't afford to pay all the difference 'out-of-pocket,' as they call it. So, Mom took up the evening shift.

On that Thursday evening, Karen and Mike weren't home. I don't remember why, maybe on dates or something. Well, only Dad and I were there. It was about ten o'clock and I was getting ready to go to bed, so I went to take a shower. I didn't notice anything odd while I was in the shower, but when I started to get out of the shower, Dad was sitting on the toilet seat in our bathroom (We call the bathroom that Karen, Mike and I share the 'Girls' Bathroom').

At first, I thought he was going to the bathroom, but that was weird because he and Mom have an 'en suite' with their bedroom. Also, he would have had to have his pants down. I'm positive he didn't.

Anyway, I had opened the shower curtains, but when I saw him, I closed them again. I asked him if something wrong with his bathroom. At first, I was just embarrassed at him perhaps catching a glimpse of me naked.

He said there wasn't anything wrong with his bathroom, so I asked him why he was using the Girl's Bathroom.

He said he wasn't using the toilet. He was just sitting on it.

I told him I needed to get out of the shower and dry off.

When he told me to go ahead, I didn't know to say or do. I was just confused.

Looking around the end of the shower curtain, I covered myself with it. Dad was staring at me with this weird expression.

I asked him to leave so I could get out.

He replied that he had seen me naked since I was a baby.

I told him that I wasn't a baby anymore. I was confused and upset, but was beginning to get scared too.

He smugly replied that I would always be 'his baby.'

I didn't know what to do, so I stepped around to the other end of the curtains and with my back turned to him stretched to reach for my towel. I had left it hanging on a towel rack that's right next to the shower. But it wasn't there.

I knew that I had left it there, but it wasn't there anymore. I was starting to get frightened as Dad was acting so bizarre.

I begged him to please leave, but he told me to not be silly.

By that time, I was really freaked out. I told him that I had forgotten my towel even though I knew that I hadn't.

I asked him if he could get me one.

He told me again to not be silly, that I should just get it for myself. I was 'no longer a baby" by my own words.

I whined that he would see me.

He just laughed and told me again to not be childish, that he had seen me naked thousands of times.

I begged him again to please leave and he just said that there was no need for him to leave. I was getting near to tears and I asked him again to please leave and let me get out of the shower.

He just chuckled and told me to just go ahead and get out of the shower, go get my towel and dry off.

Finally, I covered my labia with a hand and got out of the shower. As went over to the linen closet, I kept my back towards him as I opened the closet door, took out a towel, wrapped it around myself and tucked it in. I was more than embarrassed.

However, I had to walk by him to get to the door. I was really panicky and didn't know what to do. He was sitting there in the way.

I wrapped my arms around myself holding the towel in place in case he grabbed it when I walked by him. Of course, if he wanted to, he could have just yanked the towel off of me. There'd be nothing I could have done about it. I felt so vulnerable and helpless.

I finally forced myself to walk by him. I was trembling, but I gathered all my courage and did it. When I got to the bathroom door and started to open it, he stood up.

Not knowing what else to do, I threw the bathroom door open and ran for my room. The towel fell off, but I didn't care. I slammed my bedroom door behind me, locked it and leaned against it. I could hardly breathe I was so terrified.

I heard him walk by my door and go down the stairs. Surprisingly, he didn't try the doorknob to see if my door was locked. I don't know what I would have done if he had.

I was so freaked out that I was shaking. I didn't want to put on my nightgown. I felt like it wouldn't cover me up enough. So I put on a sweatshirt and a pair of jeans instead.

I couldn't go to sleep. I just sat on the bed in the dark leaning against the headboard with my arms wrapped around my knees. I just waited for Mom or Karen or even Mike to get home.

Finally, some time before midnight, I heard someone coming up the stairs, so I took a chance, got up and went over to the door. I stuck my head out, ready to slam it closed and lock it if I needed to. But thank heavens, it was Karen! I almost collapsed with relief.

I ducked back in my room, closed door almost to, until it was just cracked, and waited for her to come by.

My voice was wavering as I called out to her.

She stopped and asked me what was wrong.

I opened my door, so I guess she could see me with the hallway light. My eyes were red, my nose was stopped up and snot was dribbling down my philtrum (Marty told me that's what groove between the nose and the top lip is called). My face was all puffy.

I asked, no pleaded, if I could sleep in her room.

She looked at my clothes and asked me why wasn't I wearing your nightgown. She knew that I didn't wear pajamas like she and Mike did.

I didn't answer her. I just asked her again if I could sleep in her room. Even on her floor, if she didn't want to share her bed. I didn't tell her this, but I just couldn't sleep by myself, I was too frightened.

I looked up at her face and it was really pale, the opposite of blushing. She stepped over to me, put an arm around my shoulders and walked me to her room. After we went in, I closed the door and locked it.

She looked at me and I could see she was pretty angry. I thought she was mad at me, which didn't make any sense as she had just walked me to her room.

But then she grabbed her purse, yanked its strap off her shoulder and threw it across her room, smashing a picture of her boyfriend to smithereens and sending glass shards flying everywhere.

She yelled Shit! and she never cusses. I was scared out of my wits at Karen's anger and violence. I just started crying and saying that I didn't do anything! I kept repeating that I didn't do anything! I had completely lost it!

Karen started crying too and assured me that she believed me. That she was just angry, but not at me.

There were a few pieces of glass on the bed, which Karen picked up and threw in her waste-paper basket. Then she picked up the rest of the shards too There didn't seem to be any little slivers. Dieu merci! (Thank God!).

When she finished, she came over to me. I was still standing there, my back leaning against her door. She then led me over to her bed and told me to lie down.

When I did, she walked around her bed, crawled on it and laid down beside me. Then she took me in her arms and held me.

I don't know how long we laid there, but after what seemed like an eternity, we heard Mom downstairs. So, it had to have been after midnight.

She said that THIS was not going to happen again. I knew what she meant, but the word 'again' threw me. I wanted to be sure I understood what she was implying, so I asked her if it was just me. And she told me that no, it wasn't.

She asked me to tell her what had happened and when I did, she told me that Dad did the same thing to her, starting when she was ten and it went on for almost two years.

She told me that when Dad wanted to see her naked, he would just walk in on her when she was in the shower or taking a bath. Later, he would walk in on her in her bedroom when she was changing clothes.

At first, she tried to cover herself, but finally she just gave up and let him stare. He never touched her when she was naked, but at other times he was really handsy, which unnerved her because of his ogling her when she was naked.

Then, she said for no apparent reason it just stopped, after almost two years. She had stayed scared for a long time after that, but it never started back up.

However, she found out that Dad started molesting Mike when he stopped ogling her. Those were the words she used, 'molesting and ogling.'

Mike had started puberty exceptionally early, when she was not even ten. So that had made Mike his victim younger than Karen had been when he started molesting her.

Karen told me Mike refused to talk about what had happened to her, except in the most vague of ways. Mike did let it slip out once that Dad would sometimes come into her room when she was asleep (or pretending to be). She never said what he did, though.

Karen told me that she had suspicions that Dad had done more than just fondling Mike.

She said we would have to do something to stop Dad and keep me out of his clutches, but it was going to be hard. It was her way of warning me, I guess. Though, it only frightened me more.

Karen let me sleep in her bed with her and held me in her arms all night long. I hardly slept at all and I'm sure Karen didn't either.

Written during the week the 9th to the 14th of January, 1963.

Tuesday, January 15th, 1963

Mon meilleur ami du monde,

Marty, at noon, I met with Dr. Jameson and showed her the 'first day' of my journal. I was really emotional, but I didn't break down crying. Dieu merci!

This evening, when I got back to my room and read through what I had written, I saw some 'figurative language' that you might not know.

I wrote out those phrases (peu en nombre = few in number. Dieu merci!) and give them to you below. However, I think as I go on, especially as I use the 'stream of consciousness' (You probably know this, but that's a way of writing an account that tries to tell the thoughts and feelings that go through your mind as you write), I'll use a lot of 'non-literal' expressions, as you call them.

I think it will be too much for me to explain everything in letters to you. Using the phone is a problem too, as Mom is almost always around at house and I don't want her to feel worse than she already does, hearing about what happened. At school is a problem too. There's almost always a queue of girls waiting to use the phone and so, no privacy there.

I know it's asking a lot, but maybe you could get an English major to tutor you and explain the non-figurative meanings?

I just don't have enough time to do everything I need to do with writing the journal and keeping up with my classes (all of them, except ballet, being high school courses). Ballet also leaves me really tired and makes it harder to stay up late at night. (Sigh!).

It's great having the photocopier, though. It hardly takes any time to make your copies. (I'm also getting better at typing, so I don't have to make as many corrections. Also, I've figured how to use 'Liquid Paper' without having to pull the page out of the typewriter! (if the correction isn't too near the bottom of the page!).

Here are some non-literal phrases you might not already know:

1. gather all your courage [To try hard to prepare yourself mentally to do something, usually something difficult]

take a chance [To take a risk = to risk a single time]
2. seem like an eternity [To feel or think more time has elapsed than actually has]
3. walk in on someone [To enter a room and interrupt someone doing something private that they would not want you to see]
4. keep me out of his clutches [To keep someone out of the control of someone else, usually someone evil]

These make only five non-literal phrases. If there were twenty (not an impossibility), it would be difficult to 'find the time' to write everything out. (I have to think a lot about how to explain the phrases without using other figurative language!).

So, try to find a tutor. Maybe swap your tutoring for their tutoring?

I'm really looking forward to you coming up to Cambridge during Easter Break. I love our Sunday phone calls, but I still can't wait to see you! En chair et os! ('face to face').

Avec tout mon amour,
Jenny

Journal: Friday, August 18th, 1961

When Karen, got up the next morning, I was so exhausted I just stayed in bed. Though, when she got dressed and left, I did get up to lock the door. But I went right back and crawled in bed. I pulled the covers over my head and curled up in a ball. Classic fetal position. I was so exhausted physically and emotionally.

The way out of this mess came 'out of the blue.' That morning, Mom had a meeting of her charity group, the Women's Relief Society, in our home. It was involved in 'American and international humanitarian projects.' So, with Leo Cherne, the president of the IRC (International Rescue Committee), being there, it was a big deal. He talked about the IRC's work, especially about the 'Prague Spring.' But all that's not really important in my story.

However, that Mom asked Karen to help her hostess the meeting turned out to be a real stroke of luck.

Karen told me that during the tea after the meeting, Mom and Dr. Cherne huddled in a corner to discuss some fund-raising projects her group could do for the IRC.

While Mom was doing that, she asked Karen to circulate, take over her duties as hostess and make sure everyone was provided with tea or coffee and cookies and pastries.

As Karen went about her duties, she happened to overhear Mrs. Peltzer, talking about Emalie begging her to go to a private school. Mrs. Peltzer said that Emalie wanted to go to a school for girls, but when she and her husband finally agreed, they had already missed the admissions dates for the year at all the schools within a reasonable distance.

However, they found a school in Marblehead that had 'rolling date admissions.' Of course, it was Emma Hart Willard Preparatory Academy.

Mrs. Peltzer said that they had reservations about sending Emalie to a boarding school, since she was so young, but they finally agreed, doubting Emalie would be accepted.

However, Emalie took the entrance exam and was successful, it seemed. They had just received her acceptance letter. She laughed that Emalie was 'over the moon.'

Karen didn't 'let any grass grow under her feet.' By a little after noon, she had gotten the number for the school from information, phoned the school and got the Director of Admissions. Who, of course, was Dr. Jameson.

Karen found out there were two places for boarding students in the sixth grade still available for fall semester. If we could get my transcripts by the next Friday (not the that day, but in a week), Dr. Jameson said that if my grades were okay and if I did okay on an admissions exam and an interview, I could start school on September fourteenth, in a couple of weeks!

Right after the phone call, Karen ran upstairs and told me about what she found out. She said that as long as I was at home, Dad would be trying to molest me, so she needed to get me out of there.

I got that, but pointed out that private boarding schools were expensive and Dad would very likely refuse to spend the money. I was really depressed and didn't think anything could be done.

I told Karen I didn't think Dad would ever agree to letting me go. Karen, without batting an eye, said she had an idea on how to take care of that. I didn't know what to say, but I had the tiniest 'spark of hope.'

Early that afternoon, about two o'clock, Karen borrowed Mom's station wagon, telling her that we were going shopping for school supplies. Instead, though, we went to my school. When we got there, we realized we hadn't thought about since it was a couple of weeks before school started, the office might not be open.

There were only two cars parked there, but one was in a designated faculty parking place. I immediately felt depressed and in despair again and told Karen to just drive us back home.

She gripped the steering wheel and put on her stubborn face. She looked just like Mom does when she has made a decision and won't be stopped. Karen snapped that, no, we weren't giving up and that we were going to see if anyone was there.

We went to the entrance and Karen started banging on the door. She kept it up until we saw someone stick her head out of the office door. I recognized it as Mrs. Callahan, the school counselor.

Karen started waving her hand for Mrs. Callahan to come, which she did. She then opened the door half-ways and asked how she could help us.

Karen told her that it was complicated, but that I needed to change schools and asked if we could come in.

Mrs. Callahan opened the door wide for us. As we were walking to her office, she asked me how had I liked going to Hildreth and did I think I would miss it.

I blushed and didn't know what to say. Karen came to my rescue and told Mrs. Callahan I was going to go to a girl's boarding school in Marblehead. That we were going to need my transcripts to be sent.

Mrs. Callahan then asked Karen exactly who she was and I started getting anxious, but Karen told her she was my older sister. 'Cool as a cucumber.'

Mrs. Callahan looked at her doubtfully and asked her how old she was.

Karen replied that she was twenty-one."

She then lied (or rather, kept on lying), saying that Mom had a meeting all afternoon and wasn't able to come, so she had asked her to take me to school and ask for the transcripts, since time was 'of the essence.'

Karen thanked Mrs. Callahan for seeing us and told her that Dad would be traveling a lot on his sabbatical and Mom was going to be working with the IRC and would also be away from home quite a bit. So, she wanted me to go to a boarding school.

Mrs. Callahan asked what the IRC was and I had the feeling that she was skeptical about this whole set-up. She had probably had enough 'shenanigans' pulled by students over the years to justify her suspicion.

Luckily, Mrs. Callahan didn't connect me with Mike, so she didn't ask who would be taking care of her. That would have opened a whole other 'can of worms!'

I didn't know if Karen had expected Mrs. Callahan's questions and had prepared her answers, but without a moment of hesitation, she launched into her story. I was amazed at the tale Karen came up with. It seemed to have just the right amount of truth to be convincing to Mrs. Callahan.

When Mrs. Callahan asked which school, I would be going to and Karen replied the Emma Hart Willard Preparatory Academy, Mrs. Callahan was impressed and said that it was one of the best, but it was pretty expensive.

Karen 'spun out her tale' saying that I had a scholarship that would cover most of our expenses.

Mrs. Callahan congratulated me, but told us she was still a little hesitant to send the transcripts since that kind of thing was something that a student's parents should do.

But she went on that seeing the urgent need, though, and the 'fact' that Karen was twenty-one, she would go ahead and have the transcripts sent on that afternoon or the next morning.

When Mrs. Callahan asked what the address was, I almost had a heart attack, but Karen pulled a slip of paper out of her purse and handed it to Mrs. Callahan. It had the complete address with even the name of the Director of Admissions, Dr. Mary Jameson. She had thought ahead and was prepared.

Then Mrs. Callahan told Karen the cost of sending the transcripts would be a dollar, without blinking, Karen opened her purse, pulled out her wallet and gave Mrs. Callahan the dollar.

Karen was amazing. She had thought of everything!

At that moment the school secretary, Miss White, knocked on the door and Mrs. Callahan told her to come in. Miss White wanted to know about a student that had to repeat a grade. Mrs. Callahan told her she would talk to her about it later. (It was good to know she thought privacy was a 'big deal').

Then Mrs. Callahan explained my case and asked how long it would take to prepare my transcripts. Miss White asked if I had attended Hildreth for all six grades, which, of course, I hadn't since I had just passed the fifth grade! I replied I had only been there for five years.

Mrs. Callahan chuckled and explained. So, Miss White said that she could prepare the transcripts 'right away.'

Mrs. Callahan told me I would be missed and that I was a really good student. I hadn't thought about it, but then I told Mrs. Callahan I had only received two B's on my report cards. The rest of my grades were all A's. The B's were for physical ed. in the first grade. (Which was pretty lame. But I didn't say that out loud. I just thought it).

We thanked Mrs. Callahan and Miss White and headed home. I asked Karen what we were doing next and she said she would have to go telephone some people. I asked her who, but she 'kept mum' and just smiled enigmatically (mysteriously).

She told me I would find out later. I didn't know if I should have been anxious, but then I thought about Karen smiling and decided that I needn't be. Maybe…

When we got home, Karen was on the phone for an hour. Then she came upstairs to my room and told me that she would be dropping Mom off at Grandmother's at five o'clock and she would come back to pick me up by five fifteen.

After the evening from hell on Thursday, the comedy of errors on Friday evening was kind of a relief. I asked Karen where we were going and she said we were having dinner with 'some people' at six."

When I asked her who, she didn't answer. She just told me to wear something nice. She suggested my green, crêpe-de-chine trapeze dress that's the same color as my eyes, saying that it would be perfect. She also said I should wear hose and my cordovan Mary Janes the same color as my hair!

She also told me to not get dressed until she had left with Mom to take her to Grandmother's at four thirty.

I started getting ready to start to get ready, when they left. Good thing that I did, too. It took me a good fifteen minutes to find my nylons. And my garter belt which I hadn't thought about needing. (Both were on the top shelf in my closet).

By a few minutes before five, I had everything ready to put on.

I had a problem, though. I had never worn any of these clothes except for the Mary Janes. The dress, the garter belt and the stockings were last year's Christmas gifts. I did try on the dress, but not the hose and garter belt. The dress still fitted okay, aside from being little snug in the chest and hips.

Since I was a little bigger than I was Christmas, that was to be expected. At least, the garter belt would be a little tighter and not falling down from my non-existent waist to my ankles as I walked in the door of our dinner hosts.

About five, I started getting ready. I had decided on a nice pair of lime-green, cotton panties from a 'day of the week set' Mom had bought me. They were 'Tuesday's,' but I wore them anyways.

As I was going to wear the garter belt, I would need something to hide it. I needed a slip, but I couldn't wear a full one, since my dress's neckline was like a halter and the slip straps would show, so I put on my half-slip and then my dress.

This was how I usually got dressed. But then I needed to put on my garter belt. Which I had never worn before.

So, I hiked up the skirt of my dress and my half-slip up to my waist. It was hard keeping them out of the way so I could pull the garter belt up, though.

Along with much cussing (in French, as Marty had taught me a bunch of French swearwords), I finally got it up, but then started thinking that that had been stupid. I should have put the garter belt on before I put on my slip and dress. I was really getting frustrated.

Then it was time to put on my hose. Disgusted, I asked myself if I shouldn't just take my dress and slip off to put on my hose. This whole thing was idiotic!

I sat down on my bed and got more and more upset. I didn't know where Karen and I were going and I didn't know if I even wanted to go.

Dad had left early that morning before 'the hen party,' as he called it. He was going to an academic conference at Yale and wasn't coming home until the next day. One worry out of the way!

However, I started winding myself up:

I asked myself what I was going to do.

How was Karen going to get Dad to let me go?

Why wouldn't she tell me what was going on?

Should I tell Mom what happened?

If I did, would Mom and Dad get divorced?

Where was the money for the school going to come from?

How much would it cost?

What would I do on weekends?

Worse, what would I do during Christmas and Easter school breaks?

Would I have to stay at school all year without ever coming home?

Would I do all right academically?

What if I flunked out?

Did they require uniforms?

What if I looked like a twerp in them?

What if I got bullied?

What if I couldn't make any friends?

What if everybody hated me?

Had I thought of everything that could go wrong?

What was I going to do when Dad came home tomorrow?

What was Karen going to do?

Would Dad let me go?

What about Mom? Would she?

Who else besides Karen should I tell about what had happened?

My mind wouldn't stop. When I ran out of questions, I started asking the same ones over again, but they were just a little different the second time. Enough so I couldn't recognize what I was doing.

How long this went on, I have no idea. In the end, though, somewhere before five fifteen, I heard someone dashing up the staircase, but it was too early for Karen to be back, so I freaked out. Whoever it was tried to turn the doorknob, but I had locked the door. So they knocked on the door and Karen asked me to let her in. Which I did, calming down a little.

As I unlocked the door, I asked her how come she was back so soon. She replied she had just dropped Mom off at the curb and didn't go in to see Grandmother like always.

After unlocking the door, I turned around, went back to my bed and sat back down. Karen came in, looked at me and in a frenzy asked me what I thought I was doing. That we needed to leave in fifteen minutes!

She yelled at me to get my shoes on. We really didn't need to leave that soon, not from what Karen said before.

Anyway, I just sat there. Karen looked down at my legs and yelled at me that I didn't even have my hose on! After taking a deep breath and sighing exasperated, she asked where they were.

I pointed at my vanity. Following the direction I pointed, she saw the hose sitting on top of it, still in their original packaging.

Then she told me to take off my dress.

Then she saw I had on a half-slip, she told me to take off my slip too. Looking me over, she rolled her eyes at me and told me to take off my garter belt and my panties! Just to take everything off !

I was really 'ticked off' and ready to throw a 'hissy fit!'

Realizing I was 'losing it,' she wryly asked me what was I planning on doing if I needed to go pee. She told me to just think about it.

I didn't understand what she meant, so she 'spelled it out for me.' If my panties were under the garter belt, I would have to take them both down to pee; but if my panties were on over the garter belt, I would just have to pull the panties down to do my business like normal. I thought about it and then I saw what she was saying.

I thought about asking Karen to turn around, but that seemed silly. All of us girls see each other in all states of dress and undress. With us sharing one bathroom, there was no way anyone could take a shower or bath without someone needing to use the toilet. So, I just took off my garter belt and my panties and laid them on the bed.

Karen picked up my garter belt, handed me back to me and told me to put it back on and then my panties over it. Then she took the hose out of their package and handed them to me.

I sat down on the bed, dumbly holding them. Then I lifted one foot off the floor to pull the hose on and Karen shouted, "Whoa Nelly!"

She then asked me how I put on my winter tights.

I told her that I just pulled them up.

Then she asked me if I didn't roll them up to make it easier.

I replied that, no, I didn't. Then I asked if I should.

Sighing at my ignorance, she rolling up the stocking making it look like a donut, told me to stick out my left foot. Then she put the hose on my foot, and unrolled it up my leg over my knee and up on my thigh. Then she repeated the same process on my right leg.

Then she told me to stand up.

She started adjusting the garter belt so it was straight. Then she adjusted clasps, so they would hold the stockings even and at the right height. Next, she attached the stockings with the clasps.

She told me to be glad that Mom bought me a really good quality garter belt and not an open girdle with garter clasps. She said I'd be a lot more comfortable with mine. Since it was satin, it would be smooth and not show like the frilly ones did.

I asked her what was her first garter belt was like. She confessed that she had insisted on a frilly one. We both laughed.

Then she readjusted some of the clasps, stood back and looked me over.

I told her it felt weird with all the straps and everything against my legs.

She just laughed and told me I would get used to it.

Then, she glanced over at my slip and frowned. She told me my panties are nice, but my slip is awful. And anyway, that white won't do it.

She looked thoughtful for a few seconds and then 'broke into a big smile.' She took my hand, pulled me up and dragged me along behind her. We went down the hall to Mike's room. Karen knocked on her door to see if she was there, but since there was no answer, she opened the door and walked right in.

I was really anxious and asked what we were doing. I didn't want to get Mike mad at me.

Karen told me to just stand over next to the bed. She went over to Mike's chest-of-drawers and started going through Mike's lingerie. My voice squeaked as I asked what she was doing.

She said that Mike had a nice, green half-slip that was too small for her and we were going to take it.

I complained that Mike would kill me! Anyways, Mike was about the same measurement in the waist that I was in the chest. Anything of hers would never fit me. She wore a women's size 6 and I wore a girl's size 10 or 12.

Karen found the slip and pulled it out of the drawer. Then she handed the slip to me and told me to 'slip it on' and chuckled and told me that no pun was intended!

Mike's slip was beautiful. It was made out of silk taffeta; the elastic was the flat kind that didn't show or roll up; it had lace around the hem; and was made for an over-the-knee skirt. However, it was a couple of inches too big around in the waist and at least six or seven inches too long for me. It would fall to my ankles! Not really, but it felt like it.

Karen told me to try it on, but I told her that it was not only too big in the waist, but it way too long too! Then she told me to try it on anyway, but to pull it up above my breasts. I replied that like Mike always said, I didn't have any!

A little exasperated, she told me to pull it up until it was half way between my nipples and below my armpits. Then she asked me how it fitted.

I asked her how should I know how it fitted? It wasn't at my waist!

She asked if it was too tight.

I asked her what she meant.

Losing her patience, she asked me if it pinched or hurt me.

I told her I thought it felt okay.

Then she told me to sit down on Mike's bench. Which I did.

Taking a good look at me, she said that at least it didn't pull down when I sat down. She put a finger under the elastic on my side to test the fit.

I asked if I shouldn't sit down several times to make sure it would stay up.

She said that was a good idea and to sit down on the desk chair. She gave me a good looking over. Then she pushed me out of Mike's room and told me to fetch my dress and then go to her room.

When we got to her room, she tested the top hem (waist) of the slip again, pulling the elastic out and letting it go to snap me on the side (which hurt!). Then saying the fit was 'perfect!'

I asked how it could be 'perfect' with the waist above my 'breasts.'

She didn't answer, just told me to put on my dress and to sit down on the bench in front of her vanity.

After slipping on my dress, I sat down facing towards the vanity. At her wit's end, she moaned and told me to face outwards, towards her.

Looking me over again, she asked me if I had noticed how girls adjust their bras under their dresses if they were out of place. I replied that, no, I hadn't, not really. Why should I since I didn't wear one?

She reached over across her breasts pinched the top of her bra through her blouse and pulled it up a little to show me how to do it.

Then she told me to try it. I did, but I didn't feel like I could do it in front of anyone.

She told me that if the slip started to be pulled down, then to discretely adjust it. Pull it up on one side and then the other using the hand on the opposite side form the side being pulled. (overkill on the instructions!). Then she went on and told me to just not keep doing it over and over! (Obviously!).

Then she told me to look at the picture on the wall across

the room and not move my head around while she put on my makeup!

I gasped and asked her to repeat that, not believing her.

She said she was going to put on my makeup and to just hold still.

Faster than I thought possible, she put some blush, a little eye shadow (gasp!), and (brown) mascara on me. I turned around, looked in the mirror. The make-up was very understated, but it did make me look nice. (That surprised me). Then she gave me a tinted lip balm and told me to put this on for myself.

Looking back in the mirror, I put on the lip balm. Then staring at my reflection, I couldn't believe that it was me!

Karen got undressed down to her underwear, threw on a nice full slip with beautiful lace, a chicque A-line dress with a little jacket. When she had finished putting on her makeup, she had taken less than ten minutes to do everything!

She looked at me and asked herself out loud what should we do about our hair. Not giving me time to answer, she quickly combed and puffed mine out, teasing it with a comb. Then she told me to close my eyes as she lightly sprayed my hair, shielding my face with her hand.

Complaining about not having time to do our hair (what had we just been doing?), she quickly fixed her own hair, but not taking even as much time as she had on mine.

I asked her what about her hose and she said there wasn't time. Then she grabbed a string of pearls, which she put on, and then a small malachite (green semiprecious stone) necklace that she put on me.

She told me to go put on my shoes and make it snappy.

We were ready and it had taken only just over twenty minutes. She ran to the phone and made a call to a Mrs. Peltzer. I had never heard of her at that time.

Karen told her we would be a little late and that we had run into a 'few little problems' as we had gotten dressed. Then she thanked Mrs. Peltzer for inviting us over and said we would see her a little after six.

Karen ran down the stairs. In her high heels! I had problems in my Mary Janes which had less than two-inch heels!

Anyway, Karen grabbed the car keys and her purse from off of the entranceway table. Then we sped off for our dinner engagement. Luckily, we didn't run into any police. Karen didn't obey the speed limits at all!

Karen explained who Mrs. Peltzer was and said I would be meeting her daughter and could get a chance to know a little more about 'Emma Hart Willard Academy.'

The Peltzers lived in Allston on Harvard Street, so it wasn't too far away. The traffic wasn't bad at all and with the speeding, we made it to their house at five after six.

[Trying to write everything in 'indirect discourse' is a pain in the… Well, you know. I have to think what was said, add a THAT, then put the whole dialog in past tense, change YOU and YOUR and YOUR'S, to SHE and HER and HER'S, et cetera. Too much trouble!

From here on, I'm putting everything in direct dialog. I'm going to write what I REMEMBER people saying, using their EXACT words.

Well, as exact as I can remember. I may make mistakes, but I'll get close to their (and my) words if not exactly 'verbatum!'

SO, THERE!

Written the 16th to the 21st of January, 1963.

Tuesday, January 22nd, 1963

Cher Marty,

I only have time for a short note. To answer your question: No, it's not too much trouble to send you copies of my journal and I really want you to read it. The few things we've talked about have really helped me! Your encouragement always helps me.

Two 'to helps' in consecutive sentences. Not good! My teachers are sticklers. (If you don't know that word, look it up or ask your English tutor!). Anyway, they're sticklers for word precision and diversity. I've been using 'Roget's Thesaurus' a lot.

Anyway, I also was really happy that one of your tutees is an English major and has agreed to exchange time with you to explain the 'non-literal' language. I think that just reading the phrases to her instead of letting her read the text is a good idea too.

However, she'll probably 'figure out' (You know that idiom) what the journal is about. Is she trustworthy? Would she treat the information as private? Do ask her to!

Bye for now. I've got to get to my readings for World Religions.

Je t'aime!
Jenny

Journal: Friday, August 18th, 1961, 6 P.M.

Dinner with the Peltzers

When I got a look at the Peltzer's house, I was completely blown away. It was huge! It had a wrap-around porch and an eight-sided tower; the exterior had light green, patterned, wood shingles that looked like fish scales; and the trim was a contrasting rust red. It seemed like there were gables, bay windows and dormers everywhere!

Over the French (double) front doors, there was a huge, semicircular transom window of stained-glass, depicting spotted fish (salmon? or trout?) jumping up a cascade.

We sounded the doorbell and Mrs. Peltzer and her daughters came to let us in. Mrs. Peltzer was really jovial and outgoing. The daughter my age was standing a little behind her younger sister with her hands on her (sister's) shoulders. Mrs. Peltzer greeted Karen and Karen, in turn, told her that it was good to see her again! (Again? I asked myself).

As Mrs. Peltzer invited us in, Karen introduced me and Mrs. Peltzer introduced her daughters. The daughter my age was Emalie and her younger sister was Heike. We all shook hands in the foyer. Very formal.

It was really strange that Emalie and Heike both had green eyes, though they weren't as green as mine. They had some golden flecks in theirs. But their hair was pretty much the same color as mine. Emalie was just my height too. Weird!

The girls both were wearing trapeze sundresses like their mother's (and mine), though none of the fabrics were the same. (Theirs were floral, while mine was a solid, forest green).

Anyways, Mrs. Peltzer led us across the foyer, which took my breath away. It had polished oak floors and a long Persian carpet that ran its entire length. There was a sideboard along the wall that was made of a beautiful dark brown/black grained wood. Its legs were cabriole (the curved ones that have a kind of S form).

On the left-hand side of the foyer about half way down it towards the stairs was the door to the parlor.

My breath was taken away again. The furniture was

gorgeously upholstered in somber brocades or leather. There was a big couch made of cordovan leather facing into the parlor with a sofa table behind it on the foyer side.

The sofa table was made of the same wood as the sideboard. There were two, button-tufted wing chairs. Mr. Peltzer was sitting in one with his legs crossed and his feet resting on an ottoman that matched the sofa.

When we walked in, Mr. Peltzer got up and came over to greet us and welcome us to their home. He told us to please have a seat and Mrs. Peltzer asked us if we would like something to drink. She told us she had Cokes, ginger ale, sparkling cider and, of course, sparkling mineral water. Emalie and Heike asked for cider, so I followed their lead.

I wasn't sure how to act. I had never been to a big dinner except at our reunion and that wasn't the same for sure. As I was to find out, this was a formal dinner party. Something I certainly had never ever been too!

Mr. Peltzer asked Karen if she would like some wine and told her they had a nice Clos d'Église or a Huet Vouvray. She said she'd take the Vouvray. I raised my eyebrows at that and asked myself if she even knew what that was. Marty would probably know, though.

I told Mr. Peltzer how beautiful I thought his house was and he said I should have seen it ten years ago. It was a disaster. It hadn't been kept up since before World War Two began and they had to do endless repairs. With it fixed up, though, he said he thought that it might end up as a National Historic Landmark.

He said that it was built in 1882 and that Henry Hobson Richardson was the architect.

I told Mr. Peltzer I didn't know anything about him.

Mr. Peltzer replied that along with Louis Sullivan and Frank Lloyd Wright, he was recognized as one of the Trinity of American architects. He had designed Trinity Church here in Boston, the State Capitol of New York and Sever Hall at Harvard, as well as numerous other important buildings and 'residences.'

I told Mr. Peltzer that I had never heard of him, but, "I do know about Frank Lloyd Wright. He built 'Fallingwater' during the Depression."

[Uh-oh. Direct Discourse! Oh merde! (Oh crap!) Sorry! I'm just going write what seems the most natural, mixing up direct and indirect. One of the Brontë sisters, I'm not! SO THERE! [Again. Sigh!]

Mr. Peltzer nodded and said, "Yes, in 1935."
I guess it was showing off, but I sort of cut in with, "At Bear Run, Pennsylvania."
He chuckled and said that then I could understand what a find their house had been for him and his wife. A house designed by someone on the same level as Frank Lloyd Wright!
Mr. Peltzer went on and told me it wasn't just the building that was a find. A lot of the furniture had been left, stored in the basement and in the tower garret.
He said he really had a dilemma, though. He knew that refinishing the furniture ruined their value as antiques, but they were in such bad shape that their value before they redid them was questionable.
So, he said he just 'held his nose' and went ahead and had it done. But he was able to find an artisan who did work for museums and had the pieces "restored to their original condition."
I told him that they were beautiful, but that I couldn't recognize the black and dark brown wood they were made of. He told me that while a good portion of Queen Anne furnishings were made of mahogany, all this furniture was made of walnut and none of it was veneer! It was all solid walnut!
He told me that except for those pieces, Mrs. Peltzer had handled the interiors. He said that there was a lot of plasterwork to be redone, especially the pilasters and bas-relief cornices.
I told him I didn't know what pilasters were, so he told me to look at the false columns in the corners. That they were called pilasters.
He said that Mrs. Peltzer oversaw all the artisans' work and she also had selected of all the fabrics for the upholstery (leathers and brocades), the curtains (heavy velvet) and lace and their decorations like the tassels that dangled from the curtain

tiebacks, the tapestries for the walls and the Oriental and Persian carpets.

I said that the house was amazing and that the furnishings were gorgeous. Trying to impress him (again, sigh!), I asked him if the photos on the walls were Ansell Adams.

He said that they were and went on and told me about the other pieces of art.

He told me that in addition to the three photos by Adams, they had a lithograph by Picasso and a landscape oil by John Singer Sargent. He told me that the authenticity of that painting, however, hadn't been firmly established.

He told me the portraits of him and his wife and the one of Emalie and Heike were painted by Richard Estes that last year.

I told him they looked like three huge color photos!

He explained that, no, they were hyper-realistic oils done by hand.

I exclaimed that they were amazing! (I realized that I needed to stop using 'amazing' and think of a synonym).

The Peltzers had a number of sculptures. One of them looked like a Frederic Remington.

When I asked if it was a Remington, he replied that, yes, it was. He complemented me on being quite knowledgeable about art for an eleven-year-old. (I wondered how he knew my age).

I quickly told him that I really enjoyed visiting art museums and galleries.

At that point, Mrs. Peltzer came back with all our drinks on a tray and served them. She asked if Johann (she pronounced it, Yohawn) had been boring us, talking about the house.

I told her, not at all, that their house was amazing! (Immediately, I thought, Oops! 'Amazing' again!).

Mrs. Peltzer smiled warmly at that. Then she turned to Karen and asked, "How is the matriculation going?"

Karen said that everything was in the works. That the school counselor of my old school would be mailing off my transcripts on Monday.

Emalie asked if I would mind telling her what my grades were.

I told her that made two B's and all the rest were A's.

She asked me what I was taking this year and I told her that

I was taking English, Pre-Algebra, General Science, Geography, and P.E.

When she asked which ones I got B's in, I told her, "I made all A's this year."

She looked confused and said that she didn't understand.

I giggled when I saw what her problem was and explained that I had made the two B's in first grade, but since then all my grades had been A's.

Emalie turned red and told me that she didn't think I would have any problem getting into Willard.

Mrs. Peltzer laughed and asked me how come I didn't get all A's in the first grade.

It was my turn to be embarrassed. Turning as red as Emalie had, I explained, "Both of the B's were in P.E. They wanted me to do all these stupid tumbling exercises and I was null in that kind of stuff. So I got permission to substitute swimming and it turned out that that was my sport. I joined the Cambridge YWCA swim team and pretty consistently was one of their top swimmers in my age group."

Mrs. Peltzer chuckled and said, "Good for you!"

I knew something was going on, but I couldn't figure out what.

Emalie asked me what did I do during P.E. time.

I explained, "I use the time to do homework or work on individual study projects my teachers assign me."

Emalie asked which school I went to and when I told her Hildreth, she grimaced and said. "That's not fair!"

I asked what she meant and Mrs. Peltzer answered, "Emalie's grades aren't quite as good as yours and she goes to Thomas Gardner."

Trying to put right my 'faux pas,' I told Mrs. Peltzer, "I've heard that Gardner is a rough school. It would be hard to go there because a lot of its students are troublemakers." Continuing, I said, "I've heard they have a hard time keeping good teachers too."

Mrs. Peltzer said that while that was true, "A student has to do their best even when the situation is less than ideal."

I felt like I had really put my foot in it!

When Mr. Peltzer asked me why was I going to go to

Willard, Karen jumped in and said that my parents were sometimes neither at home, so I needed a stable living situation. Previously, our grandmother had stepped in, but now her health ruled that out.

Mr. Peltzer asked me what our father did and Karen told her he was a history professor and taught at MIT. I bit my tongue to keep from saying anything and hoped my expression didn't reveal my true feelings.

A woman, who I assumed was a maid, came to announce that dinner was ready. Mrs. Peltzer thanked her and told us, "We're so thankful to have Martha as our chef. I, myself, am absolutely awful in the kitchen."

She said that while Martha was there and could hear her, which I thought was very nice. To praise Martha so that she would know how much she was appreciated was nice of Mrs. Peltzer.

We went to the dining room, which, like the parlor, was beautiful. The table could have easily sat twelve. It was made of walnut too. I couldn't imagine the size of the tree it was made from. It looked like it was made of only two (very) long and wide planks that were mirror images of each other.

That's called 'bookmatched' planks. A (very) thick plank is cut down it's middle (sideways) with a bandsaw. Since the Peltzer's dining tabletop was at least an inch thick, that meant the original plank was two and a half or three inches thick and two or three feet wide! (I learned this in an individual study project. Sorry for showing off !).

Mrs. Peltzer told us who should sit where, invited everyone to have a seat and jovially apologized for her husband giving us a lecture about their house.

Karen told Mrs. Peltzer, "Jenny's interested in architecture and had an individual study project last year on the houses of the early twentieth century." I wondered how she knew about that, but realized I had probably bored everyone at home talking about my project.

Mr. Peltzer said that then I knew that their house was Queen Anne style and was probably quite knowledgeable about its architecture, which I thought was overstating it more than a little!

Mrs. Peltzer admonished her husband somewhat forcefully and he dropped whatever else he was about to say.

Mrs. Peltzer had placed me next to Mr. Peltzer, who sat at the end of the table. Karen sat across the table from me and Emalie next to her and then Heike. Mrs. Peltzer sat next to me.

The table setting was unbelievable with delicate porcelain dishes and silver tableware (of course). There were two spoons, three forks and a knife and above the plate a small fork and spoon and a small plate with a butter knife (?) on it. There were also three glasses. I knew I was going to make a fool of myself, so I decided to just watch what Mrs. Peltzer did and copy her.

I don't want to bore you any more than you already are, but let me just say that it was an eight-course meal! First course: raw oysters; second course: Avocado Soup au Café! (You could barely taste the coffee in the soup, but it was really good); third course: Grilled Cape Shark (Yikes! But it tasted really good!); fourth course: Fillet mignon; fifth course: pigeon stuffed with Indian rice and nuts!; Sixth course: beet salad with walnuts and goat cheese (and yes, the salad really does come after the entrées); seventh course: chocolate mousse and eighth course: cheeses, fruit comfits and coffee or tea. The courses were small (thank heavens), so I made it through the meal without exploding. Everything was heavenly delicious!

The adults (wrongly including Karen) had white and red wines, champagne and sparkling mineral water (so four glasses). Us kids got black currant juice, cider and sparkling mineral water (so three glasses). Really, I wouldn't have minded trying some champagne, instead of the sparkling cider!

Heike had hardly said anything all evening, so I asked her what she enjoyed doing most. She replied, "Watching television, of course!"

Emalie groaned. But Heike ignored her and went on. Complaining she only got to watch an hour each evening, she told me her favorite shows were: 'The Alvin Show' and 'Lassie'. She also watched some Disney programs, which were 'Okay.'"

I asked which Disney programs and she replied, "'Davy Crocket' and 'Daniel Boone', but 'Zorro' is better!"

Then I asked Emalie if she watched any television. She

replied, "Of course!" Of course!

Her Mom commented, "Unfortunately, too much."

I asked Emalie which programs she liked best and she said she had liked 'Ben Casey,' but now she liked 'Dr. Kildaire' better. She complained that it was too bad they were on at the same time, though.

I asked her what else she watched and she grinned and replied, "'Twilight Zone' and 'Perry Mason' and 'The Defenders.'"

Mr. Peltzer commented that 'Perry Mason' was ridiculous, but 'The Defenders' was actually quite good, except that no one law office would ever have that many interesting and challenging cases.

I asked him, "Why not, couldn't someone specializing in civil rights have that many?"

He said that he and his wife had only had a handful of cases like those and that they had been defense lawyers for over twenty years.

He then asked me was I interested in civil rights. I started to answer, "Yes and I have…"

Emalie interrupted me grinning and continued my sentence, "…done an individual study project on them."

I blushed, but I also laughed. Mrs. Peltzer, however, frowned and told her, "It's not polite to interrupt, Emalie."

I told her, "No, that's okay. I am sort of a nerd. Not like the one in Dr. Seuss, rather the egghead type."

I asked Mr. Peltzer if he watched television and he replied, "Yes, I do. It's a way to relax and unwind."

When I asked him what he watched and he chuckled and replied that he only watched Westerns.

I asked him, "Why not The Defenders?"

He laughed again and told me, "I get enough of that at the office."

I asked him, "What programs do you watch, then?"

He replied, "'Bonanza', 'Gunsmoke', 'Have Gun Will Travel' and 'Rawhide.'"

I grinned and asked him, "Did put them in alphabetical order on purpose?"

He gave a big belly-laugh and replied, "You caught me! I

always have ready answers for likely questions at cocktail parties and such. Small talk, you know.”

At that everyone had a good laugh.

Then I asked Mrs. Peltzer, “Do you watch any television?”

She replied, “No, not really.”

With a little smirk, Emalie asked her, “What about ‘Ozzie and Harriet’?”

Mrs. Peltzer laughed and said, “Emalie got that right. I do like to keep up with the Nelson Family.”

It was a long meal and we talked about everything from the Cuban missile crisis to sports to the imprisonment of Nelson Mandela, which Mr. Peltzer was surprised that I knew about.

We talked a lot about civil rights, the death penalty, school segregation and integration. Karen took up the conversation when we got to sports. All I know about sports is competitive swimming. It was ‘wide-ranging’ (in ‘posh’ terms) and to be truthful, a fun confab (or in ‘posh,’ conversation).

After the meal, Emalie asked, “Can Jenny come up to my room?”

Karen replied that since it was getting late (it was only nine thirty, though), that we really needed to get back home. She explained, “I have to pick up my mother from my grandmother’s house.”

I started to say that Mom didn’t expect her ‘til midnight, but thought better of it. However, I did beg her to just let me run up and see Emalie’s room. She gave in and said, “Go ahead, but for only ten minutes and I mean only ten minutes!”

Emalie grabbed my hand and dragged me up the stairs as fast as I could go in my midcalf length dress. Then we had to go up another set of stairs (steep ones) to get to her aerie on the top floor.

She had a big room. Her furniture was all antiques: a dressing table; cheval floor mirror; flattop, high chest-of-drawers; a low boy chest of drawers; a huge armoire and, most impressive of all, a big canopied bed with a gorgeous wooden headboard carved like flowers.

We just had just been there a few minutes and I heard a little tinkling bell. Emalie explained that was part of getting permission to have the garret as her bedroom. It meant that we had to go directly back down stairs.

Karen and I took our leave and left for home. I was worried about Karen driving after drinking all that wine, but she did okay. I couldn't tell that she drove any different from usual.

When we got home, Mom, of course, wasn't there and wouldn't be until Karen picked her up at midnight. Mom usually took the station wagon, but Karen had told her she was going to pick her up after she got back from "an evening with some friends."

Karen followed me up to my room, came in and sat down on my bed. She told me to go ahead and get ready for bed. I undressed, pulled my nightgown out from under my pillow and put it on.

Karen asked me to come over and sit next to her. When I sat down next to her, she turned sideways and crossed her legs facing towards me. I did the same facing her.

Her face got really serious and she said that we needed to decide what to do when Dad got home from his trip that next evening.

I asked her what she meant.

She said I needed to decide whether or not she or I, or both or neither of us, were going to tell Mom about Dad.

I asked her, "Do you think Mom will divorce Dad if she finds out?"

She replied, "That would be a distinct possibility, even a probability."

I told her, "I don't want to be the reason that they get a divorce."

Even as I wrote this, I knew what Dr. Jameson would say that I couldn't be responsible for what my parents did.

Karen said exactly that. "Jenny, this is all on Dad. He's the one in the wrong and not you or Mike or me."

I asked, "Would Mom believe me. Dad could say I was making it up or blowing innocent joshing all out of proportion."

Karen answered, "If Mom doesn't believe you or believe how serious this is, I'll tell her about what Mike and I have lived through. It might be better if we don't have to, because Mom would feel dreadful and blame herself for not seeing what has been going on!"

At that, I realized that I didn't want to say anything about Dad's abuse to Mom.

Karen, not grasping that my decision had been made, continued, "But if my plan doesn't work, we will be left no choice except to tell Mom, and probably, the police too."

Suddenly, I couldn't help myself. I started to cry. Karen scooted over to me and held me in her arms. It took me a while to calm down, but finally after fifteen minutes or so, I did.

Karen suggested that I sleep with her again. I told her that would really be nice, but I didn't want to bother her. She said that it would be fine. That she was worried about me.

I started crying again, but softly. She stood up, pulled me up too, put her arm around my shoulders and guided me to her room. My eyes were too blurred by my tears to see where I was going.

So, we went to her room and I crawled in her bed and immediately fell asleep because I was so 'emotionally drained' (to use Karen's words).

I didn't know when Karen went to pick up Mom nor when she got home. I didn't even wake up when she crawled in bed with me.

Written the week of the 23rd to the 28th of January, 1963.

Monday, January 28th, 1963

Dr. Jameson,

Just a note. I realize I have spent a lot of time on the evening of the dinner party at the Peltzers, but it was a good thing that came out of everything.

Also, it gives you some information about Karen's and my relationship as sisters. I guess also a little about Mike and me too.

What's more, it's a peek into my nerdy life, my complete lack of experience in social settings (all I know is what I've read about in novels) and lastly… Well, there is no 'lastly.'

We'll talk about it tomorrow.

Sincerely yours,
Jenny

Journal: Saturday, August 19th, 1961

Saturday morning was almost like any other. Mom got up and fixed us breakfast and we lazed around the house. I went back up to my room and read. Emily Brontë's 'Wuthering Heights.' Karen made several phone calls, about what I don't know to this day. She's never told me.

When Dad got home early at a little after one, Karen, Mom and I were eating a light lunch of sandwiches and a salad. Dad kissed Mom on the cheek, went over to Karen who was sitting there stony-faced and patted her on the shoulder. He started to reach out to me, but I got up and walked away, leaving my unfinished lunch.

Mom asked me what was the matter and I said I just wasn't hungry any more. As I headed for the stairs, Mom asked what was going on. Dad spoke up and told her I was mad at him.

Mom asked him why and he answered, I was just 'at that age.'

He said he hoped I wouldn't turn out like Mike. Mom told him to not say things like that in front of us kids.

Karen told me later what had happened. She said she felt like her eyes were shooting daggers at him. He glanced over at her and had to have realized that she knew.

He told Mom that he would be in his office, and she asked him didn't he want to eat.

He replied that he didn't eat breakfast and got so hungry he bought himself a hamburger to eat on the way home. So, he was okay.

Karen finished her lunch and then went to talk with Dad. When she walked into his office, he looked up from his desk and asked her if I had said something to her about him.

She asked what would I have to tell her about him. It wasn't anything that she didn't already know about.

He said that what had happened between the two of them was a long time ago.

She responded that what had happened between him and Mike wasn't all that long in the past and what he did to me was only two nights before.

He grimaced and asked what had I told her.

She just ignored his question and stared at him in disgust.

Then he asked again what had I told her, raising his voice.

Karen told him to be careful or he might attract Mom's attention.

By this time, he was fuming, but he shut his mouth and his jaw shifted like he was grinding his teeth.

Karen put her palms down on his desk and leaned over towards him. She called him a pile of shit and told him to keep his mouth shut and listen carefully.

He started to say something, but she told him he had one chance, so he had better listen or else she would keep the appointment that she had made with the MIT Dean of Faculty on Monday.

He asked her how she had gotten this 'so called appointment.'

She told him that she called the dean's secretary and told her that she had information about a member of the faculty raping a fourteen-year-old girl.

He was startled and started to look afraid. He asked what Mike had told her. He realized that he had just made a sort of confession, not recognizing it until it was too late.

Karen sneered, "Thanks for the confirmation!"

He told her that no one would believe her and that anyway MIT regularly gets such accusations against faculty members for such things.

She asked him, "But do they give tenure to anyone who has such an allegation hanging over his head? Anyway, I'm sure the police would be interested about such allegations on the testimony of three victims."

THAT got his attention.

He asked what she wanted.

She told him she wanted only two things: One, that he would pay the tuition for me to attend a girl's college prep, boarding school.

"How much…" he started to ask, but Karen cut him off and told him that if he interrupted her one more time, she was walking out of the door to first go tell Mom and second, to go to the police and report an incestuous statutory rape of a fourteen-year-old! Then she asked or was it a twelve-year old. She said that she was sure that Mike was angry enough to help out if it would put him in behind bars for a long time!

He turned ashen white, but kept his mouth firmly shut for the rest of Karen's talk.

Karen went on by telling him he would pay the tuition for me to attend a girl's college prep, boarding school and he would work out his schedule so he was NEVER at home when I was there alone.

She told him the tuition was $2,500 a year. And as for it not being there when I was alone, she reminded him that in 1949, he wasn't at home for at least for six months. So maybe he could work out another sabbatical, leave of absence or something like that.

Karen then asked him if there were any questions.

Dad was so 'apoplectic' that for a while he couldn't say anything at all. (I know 'apoplectic' from Charles Dicken's 'A Christmas Carol'). Anyway, Dad turned sarcastic and asked where he was to come up with "That kind of money?" to use his words.

Karen replied that it was quite simple. He could cash in some of his stocks.

Raising his eyebrows, he asked, "And what stocks might you be talking about?"

She told him, "The ones in the wall safe behind the painting on the wall up to your left." She went on, asking, "Would you like a list of the stocks?"

Frowning angrily, he asked, "How did you get in the safe?"

She replied, "Oh, that was a bit of trouble. First, I tried your birthday, then Mom's, then even mine. Then, what the heck, Mike's and Jenny's. Of course, that got me nowhere. Then thinking about your 'stellar sense of humor,' I tied the stocks to dates of the stock market crashes in 1929. Both of them, *et voilà!*"

I asked her however did she know the date of the stock market crash.

"Dates," she corrected me and told me 'they' was on a test she had in economics. She remembered them because she didn't answer the question "…correctly. No, fully. I just knew it happened in 1929."

"There were these three important dates," she went on. "It began on October 24th and ended, sort of, on the 29th. The two big crash days were Black Monday and Black Tuesday, the 28th and the 29th. I tried the 24th and 28th. Then the 29th…"

"Information input overload!" I yelped.

"What?" Karen asked, not understanding.

"When Marty starts 'waxing eloquent,' he told me to say that. It's from this psychologist at the University of Michigan," I told Karen to which she responded chuckling, "Information Overload!"

"That's Information INPUT overload," I corrected her.

"Yeah, that," she laughed and then went on, "Anyway, it was 10, 29, 19, 29. Black Monday."

When she said 'Black Tuesday,' she said Dad's bottom jaw dropped and he started opening and closing his mouth like 'a Japanese carp.' Not surprising, seen how Karen had in a 'streak of genius' arrived at the combination!

Then she warned him, "If you get the combination changed or sell more of the stocks than is needed to pay Jenny's tuition, I'm going directly to the police!"

Then she asked him, "Do you understand?"

He mumbled back, "Yes, I do," quite defeated.

"Oh," she continued, "the first installment, $1500 is due on the first of September, so you had better get with it and see which stocks would be the best to sell right now."

Then she told him, "And give me a list of the stocks you sell and for how much and I'll check that against my list and the New York Times's stock reports."

She asked him again, "Do you understand?"

Humiliated, he mumbled, "Yes, I understand."

She told him, "Speak up!"

He growled, "Yes, I understand!"

Then she told him, "There's one more thing you need to do. You have to convince Mom that this was a good idea." Then she went on goading him, "I'm sure you can come up with something. Maybe an academic angle would be most promising."

She then told him, "Jenny and I will be visiting the school sometime this next week, so you'd better get moving.."

With that, Karen walked out of Dad's office and headed upstairs to my room to tell me the good news.

Dad got right to work. He went to the kitchen and told Mom that the reason that I was mad at him was that I wanted to go to a girl's boarding school. He said that at first, he was absolutely against it, but then he began thinking and came to the opinion that with my 'excellent academic aptitude,' I should go to the best school available.

Mom asked him how we could afford it and he replied that he could use some of the stocks that he had inherited from his grandfather when he had died. They could be cashed in as needed to pay the tuition.

Mom wasn't sure and said that I was only eleven years old and that was very young to live away from home.

Dad reminded her that his grandfather was thirteen when he entered Eton in England.

Mom replied that that was a different era.

Dad suggested that she, Karen and I go visit the school I was interested in that week.

Mom said she wasn't sure and when asked how I had found out about this school and how could I get in so close to the beginning of the fall semester, he told her to just go and talk to me about it.

When Mom came up, Karen was in my room. We basically told her truth except for why I wanted to go and (of course) about our extorting him. I used the academic angle like Dad suggested. (Karen had given me a 'heads up' on that before Mom came up).

When Karen mentioned that it was Mrs. Peltzer who had told her about the school, she got a funny look on her face.

Karen asked her what was the matter and Mom said, "Oh, it's nothing… Only, I once knew a man whose name was Peltzer, I wonder if they are related?" Mom then said, "I've never met Mrs. Peltzer."

Karen replied, "Yes, you have. Mrs. Peltzer was one of the women who came to hear Mr. Cherne."

With that, Mom kissed Karen and me good night and headed back downstairs to get ready for bed.

Karen smiled at me and cried out, "Step one, transcripts

sent and received. Check! Step two, money for tuition. Check!" Then when she noticed I wasn't smiling, she asked, "What's the matter? Aren't you happy?"

"Yeah. But what if I flunk the admissions exam?" I moaned.

She just laughed and said, "Not going to happen. You're the smartest one in this family including Dear Old Dad!"

She kissed me on the cheek and told me, "Everything is going to be okay. You'll see. Just go get ready and come on to bed." She then ruffled my hair and told me she'd be right back 'after doing her face regime'!

After she left and I got ready and came to bed, I just couldn't get to sleep. There were so many things that could go wrong. I don't know how late it was, but I didn't finally get to sleep until sometime after midnight, long after Karen was 'sawing logs.'

Written the week of January, 30th to February 4th, 1963.

Journal: Sunday, August 20th, 1961

I just laid on the couch all Sunday afternoon and went on reading 'Wuthering Heights.' Fortunately, I was in hearing range of the telephone, so I was able to eavesdrop on the Mom's phone conservation.

Mom had called Mrs. Peltzer and talked with her about the school, us kids (Mom's and hers) and then the IRC, for more than an hour. Thank heavens Mrs. Peltzer didn't mention anything that would have revealed what Karen and I had done behind Mom's back!

I overheard Mom saying, "My husband, John, and daughter, Jenny, researched about Willard Academy." Which was half true anyway. But then I guess it wasn't really true at all, since Karen had done all the research.

Mom told Mrs. Peltzer, "Jenny and Karen will be going for a visit to the campus this week."

Mrs. Peltzer then suggested, "Why don't we all go together and make a day of it? After all, it's only 25 miles away. We could do some shopping, have a nice lunch and pick up the girls' uniforms."

Of course, I couldn't hear what Mrs. Peltzer was saying, but Mom told me all about it later. Probably verbatum!

When she relayed the bit about our uniforms, I thought, 'Yuck! So, we do have to wear uniforms!'

Mom and Mrs. Peltzer decided to go that next Wednesday, the twenty-third.

Nothing else happened that afternoon, but still it was hard to keep my mind on the book. There were so many things that had to go right and so many things that could go wrong.

As I considered how things had gone so far, however, I started thinking everything might work out in the end.

Dad was at his office at MIT all day and didn't come home until after I had gone to bed. So that was another good thing!

Written the week of the 5th to the 11th of February, 1963.

February 12, 1963

Dear Dr. Jameson,

    This week's missive is blessedly short. We still have a lot we can talk about, though.

Yours,
Jenny

Dad was off, back to work, before I got up at seven thirty on Monday morning, which was a relief to both Karen and me.

Karen told Mom that she needed the station wagon to go shopping. I reality, we went by Hildreth at nine o'clock in the morning and requested another copy of my transcripts in a sealed envelope, so that if for some reason Willard hadn't gotten the copy, Miss White, the secretary, had sent on time, we could give our sealed copy to the Director of Admissions, Dr. Jameson.

Since Mrs. Callahan wasn't there, Miss White took it upon herself to okay the request and told Karen to come back to get the transcripts before noon. After doing some real shopping (for school supplies for herself), Karen and I went back by the school and got the transcripts.

It ended up that we didn't need the transcripts, however, because Dr. Jameson gave us a call that afternoon (which, thank heavens, Karen answered!).

Dr. Jameson said she had just gotten my transcripts. (Which was a miracle, since they had just been mailed on Friday).

Dr. Jameson went on and told Karen that she would like for me to come to the school next Wednesday from nine o'clock to eleven for the admissions exam. The multiple-choice tests that made up the exam would be graded by three o'clock and we could have the interview at that time if my test grades were acceptable.

She shared that usually it took a week for the candidates to get notification of their exam results and another week to schedule their interview. But since there wasn't that much time until school started, I could do everything in one day. That way we would have some time to gather all the 'stuff' (not her words) I would need to attend.

 She then told Karen testing fee would be eight dollars and we could pay it on Wednesday before the exam.

Karen told Dr. Jameson that we had been planning to come and visit the school on Wednesday with the Peltzers.

Dr. Jameson was surprised that we knew the Peltzers.

Karen told her that Mrs. Peltzer and Mom were both members of the Women's Relief Society and that I also was an acquaintance of Emalie's. Karen told her it would be fine for me to sit the exam on Wednesday. That we could reschedule the trip with the Peltzers.

At this point I was walking by Karen as I was going to the kitchen to get a Coke. When I heard the word 'exam,' my ears perked up. I whispered to her, asking who it was.

Karen covered the mouthpiece of the phone and whispered that it was the Director of Admissions from Willard.

Dr. Jameson told Karen that on Wednesday, she herself could monitor the exam since she would be there all day. That way, they wouldn't to have to pay a teacher to come in and do it.

Karen told her that was great and asked was there anything we needed to bring.

Dr. Jameson said that I needed to wear a skirt and a short-sleeved blouse, preferably white. The skirt couldn't be shorter than two inches above the knee when standing. That I could bring a slide ruler if I knew how to use it, but that it wasn't required.

I shouldn't bring anything else, though. No books, notebooks or texts of any kind. They would furnish all the materials needed, including graph paper, pencils, straightedges and 'blue books' to take the tests in. I didn't know what 'blue books' were, but Karen explained.

Dr. Jameson told Karen that it wasn't expected that a student in the sixth grade would be able to make anything near perfect on the exam. It would have questions from simple math to calculus. Questions from simple to advanced history, sciences and social studies would also be on the exam. There could be a foreign language component if I had studied one.

Here the conversation shifted a little, to a more formal tone. She must have been looking at my transcripts, because she said that I hadn't had any language studies according to my transcripts.

But Karen jumped in saying I was fluent in French and that I had been studying it privately since I was in the second grade.

At this point I started jumping up and down, shaking my

head no, and saying sotto voce, "Karen, no!"

Karen held out her hand with her index finger up to tell me to wait a moment.

Dr. Jameson asked what program was I in, "Was it the Alliance Française?"

Karen informed her that I had studied with graduate assistants from MIT.

Sensing there was something suspicious in this setup, Dr. Jameson asked how this had been arranged.

Karen told her that Dad was on the faculty there.

Dr. Jameson just said, "Oh, I see," and told Karen that a language test would add another hour to the exam.

She told Karen that the entire language test would be in French. Thirty minutes to read three progressively more difficult texts and to answer questions on them; ten minutes for a short 'dictée' (dictation test) and the rest of the time would be spent in conversation. The fee for the language test would add an additional three dollars to the eight-dollar examination fee.

Karen said that wouldn't be a problem.

I was (literally, but gently!) banging my head against the wall.

Dr. Jameson said that she would see us on Wednesday at nine o'clock in the morning, then.

Karen confirmed the time and thanked Dr. Jameson for the 'great opportunity' she was 'offering' me!

Then I leaned my back against the wall and slid down to the floor as Karen hung up.

"Karennn! What did you just do?" I moaned.

She chided me, telling me to not be such a drama queen and to go and get a notebook and a pen or pencil. That she would tell me all that Dr. Jameson had said. But I had better be quick before she forgot anything.

I took off up the stairs three steps a time up and then down four a time. I was back in twenty seconds.

When I got back down, Karen wasn't there. But I found Mom and her putting up groceries. Mom had just arrived back from the grocery store. When they were finished with putting everything up, Mom took a pitcher out of the fridge, sat at the table poured herself a glass of iced tea.

Karen took two Cokes out of the fridge, sat down at the table across from Mom and opened the Cokes. Handing one to me, she took a swig out of hers. Looking over at me, she raised her eyebrows as if to ask, 'What now?'

I just put my Coke down on the table and sat down next to her. Then I opened my spiral notebook and grabbed a pencil out of the mug where we kept them. I was ready to write everything down before Karen forgot.

Mom told me the school called up to tell us that I needed to take my admissions exam on Wednesday. She told me this as if she and not Karen had taken the call. Moms can be so sneaky!

Anyway, Mom said we would have to cancel our Wednesday outing with the Peltzers, however. She then said that it would work out well, though, if we all went with the Peltzers tomorrow to look over the school and do some shopping.

She must have still had her doubts, though, because she asked me (again) if I was sure that I wanted to go there.

I assured her that I definitely wanted to.

Mom just said, "Okay," and asked Karen tell us what all 'the school' had said.

Karen did a credible job of relaying the information about the exam to me, but that information was extremely distressing.

I got worried because I didn't know how to use a slide rule! I didn't know how to do calculus. I didn't have a nice skirt! I whined asking why did she tell them I was fluent in French.

Clueless, she said that I was fluent. That I listened to Radio France all the time and I read Victor Hugo in French!

I told her that Marty said my accent was 'so American.'

Then Mom told me to not take everything that Marty said as gospel. Then she asked me to consider Henry Kissinger. She pointed out that his accent is pretty noticeable (awful in my opinion).

Dad had drug me to a lecture he had given at Harvard (he's a professor there). He talked about his 'comandantur' over Hesse, Germany, and the difficulties in relief work there just after World War II.

I told Mom I didn't want to use him as a role model! Moreover, I wasn't as fluent as Karen had let on!

Then Mom looked at me seriously and reminded me that I only had to have a sixth grader's understanding of the questions and didn't have to be perfect in everything. She said that she was sure I would do okay, giving for her reason that my grades were impeccable! Talk about clueless!

She assured me I would do fine, but one more time asked if I was sure going there was what I wanted to do. That there was no use in tossing away ten dollars if not. (Eleven-dollars I thought, mentally correcting her).

I considered the option of staying in the house with Dad and replied, "Yes, I want to go there if it's at all possible."

She replied, "Okay. Then you have a test on Wednesday!"

With that, I took my Coke with me and went up to my room. I thought about phoning my French tutor, John Paul Jones, (I kid you not), and asking if he knew someone who could teach me how to be fluent (ha, ha, ha!) in 'slide ruler' in one day.

But I decided not to, thinking that if Emalie got in, then probably I could too.

As my despair lessened a little, Karen came walking up the stairs. When she knocked on my door, I opened it, grabbed her and pulled her in. Slamming my door shutting first, I asked her what was she thinking, telling Dr. Jameson that I was fluent in French!

Karen just replied that I was for a sixth grader.

I felt like growling at her!

With her usual practicality and common sense, she ignored me and told me we needed to take a look at my blouses and skirts. That we might need to buy me some new ones.

I groused that I didn't need another blouse. I had a perfectly good short-sleeved white one. Then I grumbled at her that what I needed was a nice skirt! And a slide ruler! And the know-how to use it!

She serenely told me to calm down and to just let her see my white, short-sleeved blouse.

I went to my closet, pulled out my blouse and I showed it to her. She screwed up her face in a grimace and pointed out that my blouse had ruffles down the front and poofed sleeves! And it was dingy from too many washes!

I snarled that it was the only thing I had that wasn't a polo or tee shirt! (Not quite true, but close).

She suggested that we go see Mom. So, we went down to Mom and Karen talked her into letting us go shopping for another blouse.

Mom gave us a five (!) and told us to go get something nice.

We went to Sears, Penny's and Montgomery Wards. There was nothing in my size that wasn't more froufrou than my blouse at home. Karen looked thoughtful for a minute, looked me over and grinning, told me that she had an idea.

That, as one would say, didn't bode well for me!

We went back home and up to Karen's room. She dug an old baseball cap out of her closet Then she flipped my hair up on top of my head, clipped it up with a barrette and tried the cap on me.

She adjusted it to fit and pulled it down over my eyes a little. She looked me over and said that that'd do, but that I should go put on an old pair of cut-off jeans, the baggier the better. She said the ones I had on were too feminine!

As we were headed out, Mom saw us and asked if we had found me a nice blouse.

Karen told her not yet, but that we would.

Mom took a second glance at me and frowned with a sort of baffled look, but she told us good luck as we flounced off out the door.

Karen brought us back to Sears and then took me to the boy's department!

A saleslady saw us and asked if we needed any help. Karen told her that, yes, HER BROTHER needed a new dress shirt to wear on Sundays to church. She said HE had outgrown HIS old one.

The saleslady asked what size I needed. Karen asked what would she know about boy's sizes. That our Mom had just sent her off to get JOHNNY a shirt and that she told her to get a really good one.'

If looks could kill, Karen would have been six feet under!

The lady told us that they had some really good ones, but they were quite expensive, even ridiculously so. She asked who was going to spend three dollars on a shirt for a growing boy!

Karen perked up and asked if we could see them. She told her that we would need one in white.

The saleslady looked at her with a grimace and told her drolly that that was all they came in, but to follow her.

When Karen saw the shirts, her eyes brightened up. She felt the fabric and asked what kind of cloth it was.

The saleslady told her it was a silk/cotton blend, but was 80% silk. That was why the shirts were so expensive.

Karen asked if she had one in my size.

The saleslady told her that since it was short-sleeved, we would want to get it a little big, so maybe I could wear it in the spring.

Karen said that, no, she wanted it to be a good fit for HIM right now.

The saleslady looked at her questioningly, shrugged and said, "Okay." Then under her breath, she grumbled something like, "It's your money."

She picked out two, one that looked a little big and another that looked just about right.

Karen told me to go try them on.

I headed for the dressing rooms and the saleslady called to me, "Johnny! Those dressing rooms are for girls. These over here are for boys."

I turned twenty shades of red and headed for the boy's side. Karen walked over behind me and told me she would wait for me outside. But that I should try the shirts on and come back out and show her. She instructed me to try the larger one first!

I thought, 'What the heck!' But I headed in the BOYS dressing room. As I did, a little boy, five-years-old, or there abouts, came tearing out of one of the cubicles in just his briefs and those looked like they might fall off him any second. His mother came running after him yelling, "Come back here Jimmy!" I thought, 'Is it normal for a mother to be in the boys' dressing rooms?'

I considered stopping Jimmy, but thought better of it. I didn't want him to get the shirts dirty. No telling what the kid's hands looked like. For all I knew, they could be covered with chocolate from eating a Hershey's bar!

I tried on the big shirt first and saw it was definitely too big. But I trudged out so Karen could see it. She just confirmed that, yes, it was definitely too big! Then she told me to go try on the other one.

Disgusted, I headed back in just as Jimmy's mother was dragging him back in the dressing rooms with him screaming at the top of his lungs. I stayed out of his reach as his mom pushed him back into the cubicle he had escaped from.

I tried on the other shirt and it fit perfectly, which was pretty revolting. My perfect shirt was for a boy! (Perfect, except that the buttons were backwards! They were on the right side. I had never noticed that before. Marty's shirts had their buttons on the right, while mine were on the left!).

I trudged back out and Karen confirmed that the shirt was definitely the one WE wanted.

When I went back in the dressing rooms, the Jimmy was still screaming his head off. I quickly changed back into my tee shirt and escaped from the dressing rooms as fast as I could.

We went to the check out and the saleslady told us it cost two ninety-nine. Three-o-one with tax Karen handed her a five-dollar bill and a nickel. She just shook her head and handed Karen her change. A dollar and four pennies.

When we got home, I modeled it for Mom and she gushed that it was gorgeous and asked us where we got it.

When Karen told her Sears, she exclaimed, "You've got to be kidding!"

Karen replied, "Nope!" and Mom congratulated us on doing a 'great' job finding such a pretty blouse. 'A boy's shirt,' I thought rebelliously with a frown on my face.

Then Karen told Mom she just remembered that I would also need a nice skirt and a white camisole too.

She asked if we could use the station wagon to go to Marblehead the next day so we could buy a school uniform skirt. That way we wouldn't be wasting money buying something that I would never wear again.

Mom said she didn't see why not. Then she asked if we would need any more money. Karen told her that maybe we needed a few more dollars, that we only had two left.

Mom handed her a ten and told us again that there was no

use in buying something cheap. That we should get good quality 'stuff' (not her word).

Karen agreed and said that WE had really had fun that day.

Mom reminded us that the next day we would need to be back by four thirty, so she could go to Grandmother Robert's.

Karen said that we would certainly be finished by then and repeated that she had 'really enjoyed' shopping with me. That it was 'SUCH fun!' That she was sure that we would have just as much fun again that next day. ('In your dreams!' I thought!).

I rolled my eyes and started to walk up the stairs to my room.

Then, however, Mom remembered that we had told the Peltzers that they could go with us to Marblehead on Wednesday.

Then she said to no one in particular that she needed to call Mrs. Peltzer to cancel out on our outing, I decided to hang around and listen in on what she would say. Just in case!

Mom called up Mrs. Peltzer and right after the greetings told her about my exam and reprieve (from a day spent with Emalie). Then she suddenly (in my eyes!), invited her and Emalie to accompany us that next day.

Mrs. Peltzer said that she would have liked that, but she had to beg off since she had to be in court the whole day. Mom was somewhat taken aback and didn't say anything for a few uncomfortable seconds.

Mrs. Peltzer picked up on Mom's hesitation, chuckled and asked if Karen or I had told her what she did for a living. When Mom answered no, she told Mom that she was a lawyer.

Though she was embarrassed, Mom laughed and looking at me disapprovingly, said, "No, they didn't give me that bit of information."

Mrs. Peltzer told Mom that she was a defense lawyer and had an assault case that began that next day. She said it was going to be a difficult one and jury selection was going to be critical.

That she expected to be tied up for the rest of the week and perhaps even a part of the next. Wednesday was going to be her only day off that week, as the judge couldn't be there then.

Mrs. Peltzer told Mom that Emalie had so been looking

forward to going with us since she had been really bored spending so much time at home with school out and that she was sure Emalie would be really happy to go with us.

Mom then told Mrs. Peltzer we were planning on leaving for Marblehead that next day a little after eight, so we could pick up Emalie a little before nine o'clock.

Mom went on to tell Mrs. Peltzer that I would be REALLY excited to have Emalie come with us. (That was definitely over the top!). But Mom had the habit of stretching the truth if the 'social situation' called for it.

I was sure I didn't want to spend a day with Emalie. From what I knew about her, we were 'polar opposites' in our likes and dislikes!

I didn't even bother making a comment about that and just schlepped up the stairs. (I wondered if that was the right word to use for what I was doing and thought Marty would undoubtedly know).

Anyway, I went on up to my room and tried to finish up 'Wuthering Heights' before it was time to go to sleep. Which, of course, I was unable to, since I was so anxious about everything that was going on!

Written the week of the 13th to the 18th of February, 1963.

Journal: Tuesday, August 22nd, 1961

I had no intention of getting up any earlier than I had to, but I woke up to banging on my door. I looked at the clock and it was seven o'clock. Yuck!

Karen called and told me to get up and get dressed. She instructed me to wear my nice slacks and a blouse. And my Mary Janes with a NICE pair of RUFFLE socks too!

I groaned and mumbled that I didn't want to get up.

Karen said that that was beside the point and asked if she could come in.

I yelled, "NO!" Of course.

She tried to open the door, but I had locked it. After all, Dad was to have come home last night after I went to bed.

Then Karen yelled at me to come open the door. That she was not going away. Then she whispered that Dad had already gone to his office.

I growled as I got up to go and wen to unlock the door.

I immediately headed back to bed, but Karen caught me before I made it. She grabbed me around the waist just as I started to lie down.

Chuckling, she said, "Whoa cowgirl! Time to go get a shower."

"I doan wana," I whined.

She replied that that was "… besides the point."

She picked me up by the waist, hefted me to her hip and headed out the door and down the hall to the bathroom. My arms and legs were hanging down like I was a rag doll.

When she got me to the bathroom and she let go of me, setting me down on my feet. However, when I turned around to head back to bed, she cut me off before I could escape.

"Whoa! You need to take a shower."

"I doan wana!" I whimpered.

She said, "Too bad!" lifted me up and set me in the tub and turned on the shower with just cold water! I was still in my nightgown!

I screeched at her!

She calmly told me to get undressed and hand her my (wet) clothes.

I pulled the shower curtain closed, pulled off my nightgown and panties, opened the curtains back up a little and threw my (wet) clothes at her. But I missed and they smacked into the wall and slid to the floor.

Right then, Mom showed up at the door and asked what was going on.

Karen just said that I needed some help to get up and take my shower.

Mom looked at my sopping wet nightgown on the floor and asked with her eyebrows arched up if she threw me into the shower with my nightclothes still on.

I screamed, "And in cold water!" Then sticking my head out of the shower, I glared at them both.

Mom was grinning and fought unsuccessfully to not laugh. She started softly, but her laughter grew and as Karen joined in her hilarity. They were almost rolling on the floor! Not really, but so to speak.

I squealed, "Not Funny!"

After a bit Mom and Karen calmed down and Mom asked Karen to wring out the clothes and bring them to the laundry.

Putting that off, Karen sat down on the toilet seat and waited for me to finish my shower. When I turned off the water and stuck my head out from behind the curtain; she got up, came over, took my towel off the rack and handed it to me.

I growled, "Thank you," at her.

She replied that I was quite welcome. Then she asked if I wanted her to bring me my clothes or if I wanted to wrap up in a towel or even 'streak' back to my bedroom!

I replied, "None of the above!"

She just said, "Okay," turned around and headed for the door.

I yelled for her to wait and then told her to bring me some clothes, adding, "If you please."

She replied, "As you wish, Mad-muh-wa-zell!"

When she left, I got out of the shower, wrapped myself in my towel, went over to the door and locked it. Then I dried off and started drying my hair.

I expected Karen to come right back and start banging on the door, but she didn't. She waited around for about fifteen minutes before she headed back. By then I had given up, wrapped the towel around me and headed for my room.

Just as I was approaching my door, she opened it and stepped out of my room. She had my nylon dressing gown draped over one arm and a pair of my nice panties in her other hand. Thursday's pair, they were light blue.

She handed them to me; I thanked her (again), took them and walked into my room since I was wrapped in only a towel.

I closed the door, but didn't lock it. I threw my towel and the gown on my bed and quickly pulled on my panties. I noticed that Karen had laid out all my clothes for today. My towel had landed on some of them, so I had to grab it quickly before it got them wet.

Instead of slacks, Karen had picked out a grey skirt. It was a little short and fit (snuggly) at the waist. (Was I getting fat? Nah, I had just grown a little I guessed). She had chosen a light blue polo shirt and a navy-blue blazer to go with it. (Yuck!).

I had the appalling thought that I would be wearing something very much like that Monday through Friday for the next seven years!

I put on my dressing gown and went downstairs to eat breakfast. When I walked into the kitchen, Mom looked at me and told me my hair was going to look awful if I didn't comb it out. She told me to go back upstairs and get my hairbrush.

I just whined and hesitated to obey her.

But She snapped, "Get!"

So I did. Good thing too. I heard Karen on the phone saying "…of course, Mrs. Peltzer, Jenny is really excited about Emalie coming with us. Well, good-bye! We'll see you a little before nine, then."

"I'm really excited about Emalie coming!" I told Karen sarcastically, clapping my hands together like a teeny bopper. Then I asked her what she was up to and told her I knew almost nothing about Emalie except that she wasn't a good student and liked watching 'The Twilight Zone' and 'Perry Mason' and 'Dr. Kildaire' on TV.

Karen responded that she was the only person I would know that was going to my school, so it might be good to have an ally "… entering into the battlefield of junior high."

When I asked her what she meant by 'the battlefield of junior high,' that I was entering the sixth grade. She then informed me that Willard grouped the sixth grade with the junior high. That was news to me, but I should have figured that out since the sixth grade was the lowest grade at Willard.

Anyway, she went on saying that I had been pretty popular with my classmates. To which I replied, I doubted that.

She came back with, "You weren't bullied like that girl, Matilda, who you befriended."

I admitted that I hadn't been.

Karen pointed out that school cliques could be vicious. Especially in junior high.

Then she told me something I didn't know. That when Dad was teaching at Georgetown, she went to a private school and was miserable. That it seemed like she had a target painted on her back and was the victim of endless practical jokes and even real physical harm like getting slammed into in the hallways.

I didn't feel like hearing that right then, so I cut Karen off saying that I needed to go get my hairbrush. That Mom wanted to fix my hair.

Karen offered to do it for me.

I thanked her, but told her I'd rather Mom did it.

Karen ignored that and yelled to Mom that she was doing my hair!

Mom yelled back, "Okay!" Of course!

So, we went on upstairs to my room and Karen started on my hair. Regardless of what I wanted.

As we went on talking, Karen surprised me. She said that she wasn't as smart as me or Mike, but that she did okay in school. She said she would probably go to Holyoke College, if she was lucky. She said that she was definitely not Radcliffe, Amherst and Smith material like me.

I said I doubted that I would end up at any of those. That was more Marty's territory. Well, except that they were women's colleges.

She disagreed and said that Stanford, Harvard or MIT were more likely for him. Or even Oxford.

I started feeling worried and said I hoped he wouldn't go to Stanford or Oxford.

66

Karen smirked and teased me, asking, "And why might that be? You see him every summer."

I told her honestly that I didn't want to go without seeing him for long stretches and that would be the case if he went to those universities. He might not even get to come back summers!

She said that we could talk about that later, but that we needed to finish getting me dressed to go pick up Emalie.

Karen asked me how I thought I looked nodding towards the mirror.

I turned my head to each side and looked at my hair. It looked great I had to admit.

She then said, "Then, let's put on your make up," (without giving me any choice).

I complained and asked if we had to.

She said, "No, you don't really 'have to,' but Emalie will probably be wearing some."

I gave in, saying, "Okay, then." As it turned out she was right about that.

Karen said that she would JUST put on some blush, eye shadow, and mascara.

Within ten minutes she was finished. She handed me some tinted lip balm again and told me to put it on myself. I did and slipped on my ruffled socks and Mary Janes and was ready to go.

Karen was already dressed in some nice black slacks, a gray, frilled blouse and black, four-inch (!) high heels. She gave her hair a swish and was ready to go.

Karen called out to Mom that we were leaving as we headed out the door.

Mom yelled back, "Wait a second!" She came running from her bedroom.

She handed Karen ten-dollar bill to take 'just in case.'

We drove over to Emalie's in a thoughtful silence, even though Karen had suggested that we talk about my plans.

Even though it was only fifteen 'til nine when we walked up to the door, we didn't even knock before Emalie opened it. She was really bouncy. Like I get sometimes, I guess.

She greeted us and she yelled into the foyer telling her

Mom that we were there and that we were leaving.

Her Mom shouted back for her to wait up. She came out of the dining room, which was on the right side of the foyer. She must have been in the kitchen that was off the end of the dining room.

She greeted us cordially and shook our hands. Then she picked up her purse off of the sideboard, took a ten dollar bill out of her wallet and gave it to Emalie.

She told her it was to order a couple more skirts and to pay for her lunch.

Emalie cheerfully thanked her.

Mrs. Peltzer asked Karen where she planned on eating and she replied at 'The Barnacle.'

Mrs. Peltzer told us that it was a wonderful place and the food and service were very good.

Karen excused herself saying that we'd better be going since we had a lot to do.

Emalie hugged her Mom and headed out. Karen and I in turn said goodbye to Mrs. Peltzer, shaking her hand, and followed Emalie.

I ran to catch up with Emalie and we both got in the back seat of the station wagon.

When Karen got to the there, she chuckled and said that she guessed that she would she'd play chauffeur for the day.

On the way to Marblehead, Emalie and I talked about our classmates and our school experiences, which were quite different. Occasionally, Karen would ask Emalie a question and I began to see that I was wrong to think that Emalie wasn't sharp.

When I asked her about the Willard exam, she said she did good on the math except for the calculus questions, which she didn't even try since that would have been hopeless. I asked if she knew how to use a slide ruler and she chuckled and said not at all. Then she asked if I did.

I answered, "No, I don't either."

She said she did better on the English and social studies. I said I hoped I would do well on them too, but I was really worried about the French test.

She was surprised that I was taking that, so I told her what

Karen had told me would be on the test and she said that it sounded hard.

I told her I thought so too.

Then she told me that at least that it wouldn't count against me on my admission's decision.

I told that I didn't know that.

She assured me that it didn't. She had a year of Spanish and was told about the test, but didn't bother to take it. That she wasn't the foreign language type. (I wondered what she meant by that).

I told her that that was good to know it didn't count and that that made me feel a lot better.

Then, our chat turned to music. She really knew a lot about pop music and all the bands and musicians. I asked a lot of questions, but didn't reveal my preference for classical music, especially contemporary music by composers like Barber, Britten, Copland and Stravinsky.

We got along fine and I enjoyed the drive. It took less than hour to get there, so we didn't really have time get into any deep (serious) subjects.

I asked if she was going to go home often, since the school was so near. She replied that she wasn't sure. Then she asked how about me.

I replied, truthfully, that it would depend on whether my Mom or Dad were home. Of course, this meant something different for me than it did for her.

Driving up the coast on the 129 was beautiful. The school was just off of Atlantic Avenue near Preston Beach. It was actually in Swampscott (What a yucky name for a town!).

We were planning on buying my uniforms at the school's commissary, but the clerk (who looked to be about sixteen or so) told us they didn't sell them there. That the students usually bought them from a store in New York that made the uniforms, but it usually took from several weeks to get them after placing the order. So it was probably too late to place orders there for this semester.

I was really upset, but Emalie put her arm around my shoulders and told me to not worry. That we could get uniforms made by a seamstress in Old Town. That was where she had bought hers.

The clerk told us that they were a lot more expensive there, since they were 'made-to-order' and not 'ready-to-wear' like New York. (If they were 'ready-to-wear,' why did it take so long to get them? I wondered).

Emalie admitted that they were more expensive at the seamstress, but that a girl she met when she was taking her exam told her they were better quality than the ones from New York. That was why her mother had gotten hers there.

Emalie didn't remember how to get to the shop so we asked the clerk where the shop was.

She took out a map and marked it for us. It was called 'McCaffery's Haberdashery' and was near the intersection of Washington and Essex. Karen offered to pay her for the map, but the girl told us the maps were free. The school gave them out to students each fall, even returning students if they needed one.

We drove into town on the 129, which became Atlantic Avenue. The highway then turned into a twisty, turny little street, which then became Essex Street when it crossed Washington. Just to past Washington, the seamstress's shop was on the left.

Emalie told me to just wait 'til I heard her.

When we entered the shop, we heard a strong Scottish brogue, "Whit kan A dae fur ya?" (What can I do for you?). I explained our situation and the lady said, "A tellt ya whit, A'l tak yer maezur, an' when ya paws yer test ye kan come hint an A'l mak yer hail kit." (I'll tell you what, I'll take your measurements, and when you pass your test, you can come back and I'll make your whole kit. i.e. wardrobe).

"I hesitate to ask you, but can you make me my skirt today? Or by tomorrow morning at eight thirty?" I asked her.

"A hae nae wark ta dae, sae A'l mak hit this mairnin. Come hint at wan an A'll hae hit duin." (I don't have any work to do, so I'll make it this morning. Come back at one, and I'll have it done).

"Aat wan! Wow! Thank ye sae meikle!" (At one o'clock! Wow! Thank you so much!) I said all excited and she laughed.

She took my measurements and noted everything down. As

she did, I noticed some kilts hanging on a rack. I thought they were the Stuart Black Watch tartan.

I pointed to them and asked, "Is aat tha blaick mind tartan?"

"Aye, that's richt!" (Yeah, that's right) she answered.

"Sin it's blaick, green an' blae, A thocht it wis." (Since it's black, green and blue, I thought it was), I told her.

"Fit meikle div we owe ye?" (How much do we owe you?), I then asked.

"Naut, juist paws yer test first! Gae me a call an' whin ye come hint fur yer kit ya can pay yer hail bil." (Nothing. Just pass your test first! Give me a call and when you come back for your kit, you can pay your whole bill then).

"Thank ye meikle!" (Thank you very much), I said and she laughed.

"Yer ah smaat Lassie!" (You're a smart girl) she said and laughed again.

"Guid bye! See ye at wan!" (Good bye! See you at one!) I told Mrs. McCaffery.

I turned to Emalie and Karen and suggested that we go on and have lunch. After we went out of the store, Emalie asked me what that was all about.

When I asked what she meant, she said what I had said to Mrs. McCaffrey.

I knew what she meant, but acted like I didn't and explained that after I passed the exam, she would make my whole wardrobe, but we didn't have to pay anything until then. And that she would have the kilt made at one o'clock that day.

She said, "No, not that. What I meant was how did you understand what Mrs. McCaffery said?"

Then I asked what SHE meant. I didn't want to admit it, but I had just been showing off and now I was 'putting her on.'

Emalie told me that she and her Mom had an awful time when they went to the shop trying to understand what the shopkeeper was saying. She could understand them, but they could hardly understand anything she said.

I told Emalie that I had read several books by George MacDonald in Scots. I admitted that it was hard, but told her that it had really been fun! I had gotten Dad to check out

William Grant's 'Scottish National Dictionary,' all ten volumes, from the Lamont Library at Harvard and used them to work through MacDonald's books.

Emalie told me that she had never heard of George MacDonald.

I told her that he was a big influence on the 'Inklings,' the group of writers that C. S. Lewis, J.R.R. Tolkien, Charles Williams and Owen Barfield belonged to.

Emalie excitedly said she knew C. S. Lewis. I'm sure what she meant was that she knew ABOUT Lewis. She told me (unnecessarily) that he wrote the 'Narnian Chronicles.' That she had read all of them three times and thought that they were great!

My attitude about Emalie kept changing for the better.

We went on to 'The Barnacle' for lunch, and all had stuffed lobsters. Karen had an ILLEGAL Irish Coffee (she was under-aged after all). But she let Emalie and me have a sip. I really liked it, but Emalie thought it was nasty.

For dessert, Karen had a luscious chocolate cake of which she let Emalie and me have a single, small bite each. But Emalie and I got Crème de Menthe Parfaits for dessert!

When we went back to Mrs. McCaffery's, she had the kilt finished. It was unbelievable; but she made it out of summer weight, washable (!) wool with a nylon lining.

She warned me, "Ye main wash it in cauld watter."

Emalie asked me what she had said after we had left the store.

I told her that she said you have to wash the skirt in cold water.

Emalie asked if that meant you don't have to dry clean it.

I answered, "I guess not." I told her that hers was probably the same and asked hadn't Mrs. McCaffery told her.

She admitted that she might have, but that she and her Mom couldn't understand her.

Karen commented that having it washable would really pay off over time.

I asked what else we were going to do. Were we heading home since I had all I needed to wear for the exam?

Karen said no that we had another stop to make.

When I asked what, she just told me I would see.

I whispered to Emalie that that usually meant trouble.

We headed back out of town on Atlantic and pulled up in front of Dorothy Ann's Lingerie Shop.

Uneasily, I asked Karen what she had in mind.

She told me I needed some grown up lingerie.

I asked, "And what exactly is 'grown up' lingerie?"

She told me that even if Mike let me have her green slip. It wasn't really a strapless slip. That anyway, I needed some nice panties and chemises.

I told her I had some nice panties that Mom had bought me.

She told me that she didn't think 'day of the week panties' are appropriate for junior high girls.

Emalie snorted, but when I turned and stared at her, she turned red. Still though, she couldn't quite make all her grin go away! Arghhh!

We went inside and Karen greeted the saleslady, Mrs. Reynolds, and told her that she was Karen Roberts and she had called her up the day before.

Mrs. Reynolds responded, that if she remembered correctly, Karen had said that she wanted to get some lingerie for her little sister.

Mrs. Reynolds looked at Emalie and then me and told Karen that she hadn't told her that she had twin sisters.

Emalie and I turned and looked at each other. I guess with our hair and eye color and the general shape of our faces, we did sort of look alike.

I told her that, no, we weren't sisters. Just friends.

Then she asked which one was Jenny.

I raised my hand and told her that was me.

She turned to me and said that then we should get me measured and asked me to go back into the fitting room.

I shot Karen a glare as I walked into a back room to get measured. Again! But this time for something I, for sure, didn't want. Or need!

The fitting room was pretty 'posh' as the Brits would say. There were no less than seven tapestry-upholstered chairs. Obviously antiques. There was also one of those triple mirrors that let you see the back of your head and your butt if you wanted to.

Mrs. Reynolds asked me to take off my skirt and blouse. She said I should use the changing room behind the fitting room. I thought that her asking me to strip to my panties was strange, but I went in the changing room and did as she asked.

The changing room was huge for what I thought of as a dressing room. I guessed it was needed for those women who could be called 'corpulent.' The walls had no less than twelve hooks to hang clothes on!

When I walked out of the changing room into the fitting room, Mrs. Reynolds was pulling a tape measure out of a drawer of this little secretary desk. When she turned around and saw that I only had my panties on, she exclaimed, "Jenny! I didn't mean to take off your slip too!"

Embarrassed, I told her I hadn't been wearing one.

She said she could have measured me over my clothes or given me dressing gown to wear while she was taking my measurements!

She asked me if I wanted to wear one now, while she did.

I replied to her, "No, that's okay." Feeling more than a little ill at ease, I joked, "After all, you can't un-see something!"

Mrs. Reynolds gave a good laugh and told me she wished all her teen customers were as 'sanguine' as I was. I didn't know what that meant. I was going to have to look up 'sanguine' when I got home.

She took my measurements, went over to a closet and took out a beautiful quilted silk gown just a little too big for me and told me to wear that while we picked out, "What your sister thinks you need."

I told her that she'd got that right, at which she chuckled. She then told me I wasn't alone in getting "clothing decisions hoisted on them by others." I giggled at that and decided that I liked Mrs. Reynolds.

She went out to the showroom and asked Karen and Emalie to come on back. Turning to Karen she asked, "Now what do you need?" (Why did I think of it as 'you singular?' as in Karen alone? And not 'you plural' as in Karen and me?).

Karen told her that WE wanted five white chemises, one green, the color of my eyes if she had it, and another in black.

74

She said that I'd need panties the same colors to go with them.

Not even asking my opinion, she went on to say the panties should have some lace and perhaps some insets, but tastefully done.

Taken aback, at first, I made no comment. But then plucking up my courage, I asked, "Black? Why do I need black?"

Karen replied that I'd need something sexy.

I protested, that at my age, I didn't need sexy!

Emalie gravely agreed with Karen and told me I should just go with it.

Mrs. Reynolds said she agreed with Karen too. She said that nothing helps your confidence like wearing some really nice lingerie.

"Whatever!" I said, throwing in the towel. These decisions were being made for me regardless of how I felt about them.

Then Karen remembered that I would need a strapless green slip the same…

"…color as my eyes," I finished her sentence.

Mrs. Reynolds said she didn't have anything that color, but she could dye some fabric to make some up. She said she could also sew some nice lace around the bottom hem, but it would cost about four fifty all together!

Karen told her that that would be fine.

Mrs. Reynolds brought out some rather simple nylon panties, but Karen said that they were too plain. That I needed something nicer. Needed? Yeah, like a hole in the head!

I started to say they would do just fine, but just kept quiet (after all, what did I know?). Karen would just ignore my opinion anyway.

Next, Mrs. Reynolds brought out some really fancy ones. They had a lot of lace and with panels that you could see through. Not in the middle of the front, but above so you could see your belly, but not any pubic hair (if you had any!).

I absolutely refused to even consider them, which Mrs. Reynolds grinned at. Even Karen admitted that perhaps they were "…a little too mature for me."

Then like the three bears' porridges, Mrs. Reynolds brought out some that were just right. They were nylon with a cotton gusset and had some nice lace around the leg and on the waistband.

I asked if she had any in my size and she said yes, she did. When I said I was surprised that she had them in children's sizes, she responded that they weren't in children's sizes, but rather in juniors. They would fit me in the waist and legs right now because of the elastic, but would be just a little loose. According to her I would soon grow into them. Something I wasn't looking forward to. Who wants to start having periods!

We got the white ones in that style, but the black ones were only available in the style with panels. She didn't have any in any style 'the color of my eyes.' In black, she didn't have any that fit me either, only ones that were an inch (or more) too big in the waist and hips.

I said that was okay. That I really didn't want any black ones in any case. Karen, however, overrode my veto. Again! She said SHE (meaning me) would appreciate having them soon. In black? Really, I didn't think so! Not soon. Not ever!

Mrs. Reynolds told Karen that she didn't have a chemise in black in my size either.

'How come she doesn't talk to me?' I asked myself. One of life's puzzles.

Karen asked how about one in a junior.

Mrs. Reynolds answered that she didn't have any in the smaller (-est!) juniors' sizes that I would need.

Karen then asked if she could make me a set (in black) in the same size as the others.

Mrs. Reynolds replied, "Of course." Of course!

Karen asked if she had an A bra size in matching colors to the panties.

Mrs. Reynolds countered with, "How about a double A?"

Karen looked me over (really, at my flat chest) and admitted that that might be better. She said we would take the panties and the white chemises with us right then. And the matching bras! Merde! (I don't need to translate that!). I'd had enough of all this!

Mrs. Reynolds told Karen that since she didn't have the green chemise, panties, bra and, of course, the slip in the shade she wanted or even fabric. That she was going to have to make them, including dying the fabric.

"You can make the matching bra too?" Karen asked.

Mrs. Reynolds answered, "Of course." Of course! But continued that it would cost about half again as much as the ready-to-wear ones.

Karen told her that would be fine and asked when we could pick them up then.

Mrs. Reynolds replied we could get them in a week except for the green items. Those would take at least a month since she would have to order the dye from London. The delay, of course, was because she would have to dye the cloth herself and to get the color right, she would have to dye it with Dylon Dye. Whatever that was.

Karen asked how much would everything be?

Mrs. Reynolds said everything would cost fifteen dollars plus tax and explained that she had to charge extra for the green items since they were special order.

Karen paid her. (Where did the extra money come from? Mom must have given her more money I didn't know about).

Anyway, then we headed back for Allston and afterwards, Cambridge.

When we got home it was right at four thirty. Dad was there and had just finished an early dinner. When we walked in, he immediately left for his office at MIT. It was really awkward, but Dad was keeping up his end of the bargain. Every time I saw him, though, it threw me for a loop and I felt a little sick. 'How long will that last?' I asked myself.

Karen didn't see my reaction to Dad's presence. She just headed back out taking Mom to Grandmother's.

I leaned against the wall for a while and then I headed up the stairs just as Mike was coming down.

She asked me if Dad was still there.

I told her that, no, he had just left.

Mike commented that he was hardly ever at home recently.

She looked down at me and must have seen something in my expression.

"Oh shit!" she spat and asked, "Did he…?"

I told her, "No! He hasn't touched me. He just… Well, he did what he did to Karen. But only once."

She asked if that was why I was going to boarding school.

When I told her, yes, it was, she called him a shit-faced son-of-a-bitch. Just the same as Karen told me she had.

I told Mike I was sorry I didn't see what was going on. To which she replied that I wasn't the only one who didn't.

I told her I was sorry again and started crying.

She affectionately called me 'Twerp' and said there was nothing I could have done. But at least now he wasn't going to bother me. Brightening up, she said that maybe she could work it out where he stayed away all the time or would send her to boarding school too!

Mike did something that I can't remember her doing in years. She hugged me and ran her hand over my hair.

I really started crying and sobbed, "I'm so sorry!"

She again told me I couldn't have done anything. That I was what? Eight years old? She said it would turn out all right. That at least she hoped so.

Then she did something else very un-Mike-like. She asked me if I wanted to play some chess.

I said I guessed so.

Mike used to play chess with Dad all the time when she was a kid, but she stopped when she was about ten-years-old.

She told me to go on up to her room. That she would bring us up some Cokes. Then she wiped my tears off my cheeks!

When Karen came back home, she came upstairs and knocked on my door. When I didn't answer, she peeked inside and seeing I wasn't there, went on down to Mike's room since she saw that her door was open. When she peeked inside, she did a 'double-take' when she saw Mike and I were playing chess.

"Uh, Mike," she said, "I need to talk to Jenny."

"It's okay. She knows," I told Karen.

"Oh, I see," she said and came in and sat down on Mike's bed.

Mike and I were playing pretty furiously, each making our move and tapping the clock. Mike was slaughtering me though. She still had her queen, two castles, one knight, one bishop and five pawns to my one castle, one bishop, two knights and six pawns. The game wouldn't take long.

Karen told me to not stay up too late, that we would need to leave by six thirty the next morning. She told me that Mom was going with us. She also told me I would need to wear my blue blazer as well as my new shirt and skirt.

She said we would eat breakfast in Swampscott at a café just a little ways from the school.

Mike grinned and asked Karen if she wanted a play a game of chess after she beat me.

Karen laughed quietly and said that she would only play if it was against me.

Mike grinned slyly and told me it was checkmate in three moves.

I asked her how.

She pointed, saying "Queen there, castle there and the bishop covers the queen."

I started to argue that if I took her… Then I saw the moves to checkmate and cussed, "Merde!" (Crap!).

Karen needled me, telling me that Marty was a bad influence on me!

"Or vice versa," Mike proposed.

"Okay, one more," I said to Mike.

Written the week of the 20th to the 25th of February, 1963.

February 26, 1963

Dr. Jameson,

Sorry about the conversation in Scots with Mrs. McCaffrey, but it does show a little bit more of my 'nerdy' personality. As well as some of my reading interests (C.S. Lewis and George MacDonald).

Yours truly,
Jenny

Journal: Wednesday, August 23rd, 1961

I didn't sleep well at all. I was taking my exams in a classroom full of six-year-old girls. The English exam was on the humor in the Canterbury Tales to be answered in the original language. History questions were on the legacy of Ivan the Terrible (Ivan Grozny) and its influence on Australian development. Social studies were on the development of socialism in Sweden before the Thirty Years' War. Biology was on the neurological differences between epilepsy and autism (An Essay). And best of all, the language test was on Cantonese!

Everyone in the class made 100%, but me. I made minus 13%. The punishment was getting beat on the head with a Gutenberg Bible by the proctor, who was Dad. The little girls were building a gallows for me. I heard their hammers driving nails into the timbers.

As I surfaced from the fog of sleep, I realized someone was banging on my door.

Karen was yelling that it was time to get up. Her strident voice pierced my eardrums. I looked at the clock and it was five forty-five.

I shouted, "Go way! Vas t'en! Leave me alone! Fiche-moi la paix!"

She calmly replied that my exams were that morning and that I needed to get up and take my shower.

I fell out of bed, stumbled over to the door and unlocked it. Before I realized that was a bad idea, Karen grabbed me around my waist and hauled me to the bathroom. (Again!). Then She dropped me into the bathtub and turned on the shower. (Cold water again!).

While I was in the shower and heating up from its icy start, Karen came in and hung my clothes for the day on the clothes hook behind the bathroom door. The white (boy's) shirt, a white chemise, the plaid skirt and my blue blazer. My panties and (Gawd!) hose and a garter belt that she laid on top of the toilet seat. 'No, no, no! Absolutely not!' I thought.

When I came out of the bathroom dressed, except for the garter belt and hose, Karen stuck her head out of the door of her room and saw that I didn't have them on. Obviously, since I was holding them wadded up in my fists.

Karen didn't look like she intended to fool around, so I started talking fast.

I told her that my comfort came first and I was going to wear my nice sandals AND was not wearing my Mary Janes, my garter belt, my hose nor even my blazer! I told her it was too hot and I would be dripping sweat, which wouldn't help my concentration.

I assured her that from the fourth on, though, I would wear "what the preppies wore."

"Deal?" I asked holding out my hand to shake. She looked at my hand and after several long seconds, reached out and shook it.

"Okay. Deal!" she gave in.

I told her I would go put on my sandals and we could head out.

I ran to my room, took off my blazer and tossed it, my garter belt and hose on my bed. Then I grabbed my sandals and put them on, replacing my Mary Janes.

As Karen and I were heading out, I yelled out asking Mom where she was and told her that we were leaving!

She hollered from the kitchen that she'd be there in a second. A few moments later, she came, carrying a big round Tupperware container and a big metal thermos.

She told us she thought it might be nicer to eat on the beach across the road from the school. That way, we would only be a few minutes from the school.

She said that there might be some cool onshore breezes, so I should bring my blazer and Karen should bring her grey cardigan too.

I rolled my eyes and looked over at Karen. She was making a face too. But as she headed up the stairs, I followed her. When we were about half-ways up, Karen whispered to me, "She out smarted us didn't she?"

I answered her that she got that right and we started giggling.

Fifteen minutes later, we were safely installed in the station wagon and headed up Cambridge Parkway towards US

84

Highway 1. The traffic was bad, though, and when we saw we were going to be behind a bit, Karen and I went ahead and ate our bacon and scrambled egg on a biscuit sandwiches! Mom had made English Breakfast Tea and told Karen to pour ourselves cups too. She plastic cups for us all in the Tupperware.

Mom had made us two sandwiches apiece, but I was so nervous, I could hardly get one down. The tea was nice though. It calmed me down a tad. Karen ate both of her sandwiches and the one I didn't eat too. After all, what reason did she have to be anxious?

We got to the school at fifteen 'til nine. Mom gave me a hug and said she'd wait for me outside on the bench under the maple tree. Karen went with me inside as we headed for the school office.

Dr. Jameson caught sight of us and chuckled, saying that she didn't know if I was going to show up.

It seemed strange that Karen had never met Dr. Jameson, in spite of how much they had talked over the phone (and even though she was now meeting her, Mom still hadn't).

Dr. Jameson was quite pretty with golden blond hair. She was dressed in a trim looking skirt and matching jacket. She was really tall and skinny. No, slender. She probably wore a women's size 0. Her bra was probably size B. I imagined Marty would look like a man's version of her when he grew up.

I was anxious as I explained our tardiness, telling her that the traffic through Lynn was bad and that was why we were a little bit behind.

She must have sensed my anxiousness, because she told me to just calm down. That she was sure I would do brilliantly! (very English that).

Karen said she would leave us then and wished me good luck. She gave me a hug and said she would wait for me with Mom, in front of the building.

Dr. Jameson told her that she and Mom could wait in the teacher's lounge if they wanted to.

Karen said thanks, but that it was cooler outside with the ocean breeze and that they might go for a walk on the shore while they waited.

Dr. Jameson said I would be finished at noon. Then she directed me down the hallway to the door marked 'Library.'

When we went in, there was another girl, who looked to be about sixteen sitting at one of the library's long reading tables.

Dr. Jameson introduced me to Havala Mansour. She went by Hava, though, Dr. Jameson told me. Then she told her that I would be beginning sixth grade and then in turn told me Hava would be attending the Ninth Grade.

Dr. Jameson then gave us our packets. There were two 'blue books' (test booklets) in each envelope as well as the question sheets. We would have thirty minutes to complete each test: Math, Biology, Social Science and English, in that order.

She told us to make sure we had the right test sheets when she told us to begin. After time was called, we had to hand in the 'blue books' and test sheets to her and that we shouldn't begin the next test until she told us to.

She said that especially for me, but for Hava also, that if we didn't understand a question, we should go on to the next one. The questions were not in order of difficulty. For example, a simple multiplication problem might be followed by a quadratic equation, followed by a fraction to decimal conversion.

Then she told us to take out the math question sheets from its envelope and put them face down on the table. She said we should make sure we had the rest of our envelopes in order: Biology, then Social Science, and then English, on the bottom.

Then she repeated, Biology, Social Science and then, English, on the bottom. There was also a little pencil sharpener in ashtrays in front of each of us. She told us if we needed to sharpen a pencil, we should make sure the shavings fell into the ashtrays.

She asked us if there were any questions.

When we answered, "No Ma'am," she wished us the best of luck and told us to turn over our math sheets and begin.

Hava and I were sitting across from each other and Dr. Jameson was seated at the end of the table. She used an egg timer to mark the time. It ticked really loud and, to be truthful, was really annoying.

I quickly looked over the questions. There was one calculus problem that dealt with acceleration, three binary and two ternary quadratic equations. The other questions were simple math: fractions, multiplication, long division and such. That meant the best I could do was 85% since I couldn't do the ternary problems or the calculus. That was if I didn't make any mistakes. I had taken pre-algebra, so I thought I could do okay on the binary algebra problems.

After I had finished all the other questions, I started on a ternary one, but time was called before I got anywhere.

The biology section had a number of classifications. There was labeling of the organs of an amoeba and an earthworm.

There was also a human dissection drawing where you had to label the major organs. Extra points could be earned by labeling more than where there were arrows and blanks. The body was a generic one without sex organs or breasts. Ha, ha, ha! I got twelve more items than the ten requested. That meant I would probably get more than 100%. Yeah! Well, at least on this test.

The social science was heavy on psychology, which helped since Marty and I had talked a lot about developmental psychology and mental illness. There was also cultural anthropology and sociology. I didn't think I did so well on those.

The English section was really easy. There were a lot of either/or questions on stuff like whether to use lay or lie (i.e. transitive or intransitive), as well as who/whom/whose questions. Pretty simple stuff, all in all.

The last part was writing a short essay of one hundred or more words. It wasn't necessary to finish it as long as it was correct in grammar, development and logic.

The only two sections that I was worried about were the math and social sciences.

Dr. Jameson let us run over a tad after each test, since there was a minute or two lost between the sections.

Hava was visibly exhausted. She even looked like she might be sick (as in about to puke!).

Dr. Jameson shook hands with us and told us that we should come back to her office at three o'clock to get our results. She told Hava that she could go, but me that I should remain there since I had the French test to do.

A middle-aged woman came in the library a few minutes later. She was the opposite of Dr. Jameson in just about every way. She had jet black hair worn in a bob, was curvaceous (probably a size D) and wore really feminine clothes, a gorgeous flowing summer dress with a floral design and had a silk scarf that matched the primary color of her dress, a bright red.

She walked over to me and greeted me, "Bon jour! Je suis votre surveillante à cet examen. (Hello! I am your proctor for this exam). Je m'appelle Mademoiselle Simone Prud'homme. (My name is Miss Simone Prud'homme). Vous avez trente minutes pour en finir cette section de l'examen (You have thirty minutes to finish this part of the test). Toutes les consignes sont données en Français (All the instructions are given in French). Okay, Commence! (Okay, begin!).

I thought that she was really abrupt! The exam wasn't particularly difficult, though, Dieu merci! (Thank God). There were a few words I didn't know, but I recognized all the test paragraphs/poems: 'Le Petit Prince' by Saint-Exupéry, 'Les Miserablés' by Victor Hugo and 'Les Feuilles mortes' (The Dead Leaves) by Jacques Prévert. The dictée was from Jean de La Fontaine's 'Les Fables Choisies, Le Conseil Tenu par les Rats' (The Council Held by the Rats).

When the dictée was finished, Mlle. Prud'homme and I just sat and talked. I was pretty sure I aced it.

Then I went out on the front lawn and found Mom and Karen sitting on a bench under the huge maple tree.

Mom asked me how it went and I said I thought I did okay, but that we would find out at three.

Mom encouraged me saying she was sure I did just fine.

I asked Mom if we could go to 'The Barnacle' for lunch. I was starving since I didn't really eat before the exams because I was too nervous.

She asked Karen if she knew how to get to 'The Barnacle.' She replied that yeah, we had eaten there the day before. Mom said, "Good. Then let's go!"

Like yesterday, Karen and I got stuffed lobsters. Mom, though, got a steamed one and vegetables. For dessert, we all got Crème de Menthe Parfaits. Karen wanted to order an Irish

Coffee, but Mom wouldn't let her. So, she ordered a café au lait. I thought it was a little hypocritical of Mom, since she had a big glass of wine. But I got a caramel machiatto! So, I was happy in any case.

After our lunch, we drove back to the school and got there about fifteen 'til three. Hava and her Mom were already there, waiting for Dr. Jameson to finish grading our tests.

While we waited, Mlle. Prud'homme came out of the office and told me that I made a 3.91/4.00. I had only missed one plus-que-parfait du subjunctif and one passé antérieur. I had a perfect on the dictée. She said if I could improve my accent, I could have a native speaker status! (This was actually funny since her English had such a strong French accent!).

While Mlle. Prud'homme and I were talking (in French), Dr. Jameson exited her office. She called Hava and me over and told us that she and I had pretty close to the same raw score. Me, a 2.95/4.00 and Hava, a 3.05/4.00. I was really upset and almost felt like crying.

When Dr. Jameson saw my face, she told me I didn't understand. That what she had given me was what my grades would be if I were a senior in high school taking the exams for an international baccalaureate!

She explained that since I was just in the sixth grade, when the grades were weighted, I would have much higher than four point. The grades were weighted inversely to one's age or grade in school. Actually, if I had made just a little higher grade, I could have had an international baccalaureate degree right then. And that was not taking into account my French exam grade.

She said that if that was included, I could have an International Bac. Right then. She said, however, she wouldn't encourage that. She said I should give myself time.

She said that at Willard, I could take any course that I passed the prerequisites for. That could be by taking the courses or by passing an exam. When I had 'eaten' up all the possibilities including independent studies, then I should consider going on to university.

She told me I was one of the most intelligent girls that had applied in recent years, but I needed to give myself time to mature emotionally.

I thanked Dr. Jameson and told her I thought I had messed up and flunked the tests.

She told me that, no, I had done well enough to earn a full scholarship if I had the economic need. She was sure the board would give me one if that were the case.

I told her that I didn't need one right then, but there was a possibility that I might need it in the future."

Looking concerned, she asked if I foresaw my circumstances changing in the near future.

I told her I really couldn't talk about it.

She responded she wouldn't invade my privacy, but if I needed to talk to someone, her door was always open. I looked over at Mom and hoped she hadn't heard what I had said.

To avoid going further down that road, I asked Dr. Jameson to let me introduce her to Mom.

After I did so, Mom told her it was nice to finally meet her and they shook hands.

Mom said that she was happy that I would be studying there at Emma Hart Willard Preparatory Academy. That it was a weight off her mind.

Dr. Jameson told Mom that she looking forward to having me with them the coming semester.

She said I would be living in the Susan B. Anthony Dorm. That was where the first, second and third years resided.

Then she turned to me and asked if I would like to know the names of my dorm mates.

When I eagerly replied yes, Dr. Jameson said she could look them up for me. That they were on file in her office.

I thanked her, so the four of us, Mom, Karen, me and Dr. Jameson went to her office to get the dorm assignment file.

Dr. Jameson pulled the file from a folder in a filing cabinet and told me I would have a room in one of the quads. That is, one of the four-student suites.

She explained that each girl got her own room off of a common room. She told me that my room was number twenty-seven C. and that I would be rooming with Sarah Greenberg, she was in twenty-seven A, and Emalie Peltzer, who was in twenty-seven B. Room D hadn't been assigned yet and might not be that semester or even that whole year. That would give us girls some extra storage space.

She said we would be on the second floor and I was actually quite lucky as I would have a corner room with views of the beach and the woods.

Mom asked if it would it be possible to take a look at my room so we could see what I would need in terms of curtains and linens.

Dr. Jameson replied that she didn't see why not. She said she would need to get the master key and then we could go see my new home for the year.

Dr. Jameson went in a room off her office for a minute. You could hear the metallic sounds of a metal locker being unlocked, opened, closed and relocked. She came back to her office and asked us to follow her.

Then she directed us to Anthony Hall which was on our right as we exited from the front lobby. The dorm building faced north. My room, she said, would be on the south-east corner of the building.

Mom walked next to her and engaged her in a talk about the problems she faced being responsible for a couple of hundred students.

Dr. Jameson said she had 159 students this year; 160 was full enrollment. They had rooms for 100 residential students. Sixty-four were reserved for high school students and thirty-six for junior high students. At present, only one room was unassigned; that was the empty room in my quad.

The junior high students lived in the quads, where four rooms shared a common room. The senior high schoolers lived duplexes, where two rooms shared a study/lounge.

The senior high students had eight fully equipped kitchens with eight girls assigned to each. Junior high schoolers weren't allowed to cook in their dorm, but they did have a refrigerator in each common room to store sodas and perishable food.

She told us that the reserved sixty places for day students never had any problem being filled. It was more of a problem to fill the rooms for residential junior high students because, unlike the British and other Europeans, Americans were unaccustomed to having students in residential schools until the children were fourteen or older.

The selection process for Willard was rigorous; they accepted about the same percentage of applications as Wellesley, which ended up being about 30%. The exit exam for Willard required a 3.25/4.00 for the International Bac. That was equal to a 2000/2400 on the ACT. The entrance exam for Willard required a 3.00/4.00 to even be considered. Grade point averages from public schools were considered, but 'cum grano salis' (with a grain of salt). Of importance also were the psychological and social profiles of the prospective students.

Dr. Jameson excused herself for being so boring about such 'arcane' administrative information, but that it was a part of her role as Director of Admissions, along the with academic counseling and psychotherapy.

Surprised, Mom asked if she was a psychologist to which Dr. Jameson replied, "Well yes, I am, though I don't have a PsyD, a doctorate in psychology. That's the usual degree for psychologists."

"Then you have an PhD in psychotherapy? Is there such a thing?" Mom asked and then continued, "I know very little about degrees in medical fields. I just know a psychiatrist is a MD and a psychologist isn't. My husband's career is more academic than practical, but I would never tell him that!"

"Well, to answer your question, there is a PhD in Counseling Psychology among many other flavors. My PhD is in Clinical Psychology, but I did a study on client-centered therapy."

"Does that qualify you to do psychotherapy? Sorry, that didn't sound respectful. I didn't mean to be rude. I'm just interested."

"No, that's fine. My PhD does qualify me for psychotherapy as a Psychologist, as well as another of my degrees," Dr. Jameson answered chuckling.

"Degrees?" Mom asked.

Dr. Jameson grinned and explained, "My educational trek is a little twisting and turning. It started with a Bachelor of Science in Nursing from Columbia University and a Master of Science in Psychiatric Nursing at Rutgers University. Then I got

92

my PhD in Psychology at the University of Minnesota, where Carl Rogers was my advisor." (It was only later that I understood the significance of Carl Rogers being her advisor. As he was the father of client-centered therapy!).

Dr. Jameson laughed and said, "Quite an alphabet soup!"

Mom exclaimed that Dr. Jameson couldn't be old enough to have all those degrees!

Dr. Jameson thanked her, but said she was probably older than Mom thought. That her schooling went on for almost twenty years after her high school graduation! Though, a number were clinical hours, actually working! ('As though university and graduate school wasn't work,' I thought).

Mom confessed that she was really impressed that a school as small as Willard could attract someone like her.

She replied that she really enjoyed her work there, in part because of its variety. "I wear quite a number of different hats. Director of Admissions, Academic Counselor, Psychotherapist and School Nurse!"

"School nurse? Oh, your bachelor degree from Columbia!" Mom asked and then answered her own question.

"Yes, I've maintained my RN status as well as that of psychologist. Excuse me again. I'm seem to be running off at the mouth this morning."

"No, not at all, I'm really impressed with all your training and education. Just let me say, Willard is lucky to have you!"

"That's very kind of you to say," Dr. Jameson replied.

As we got to the entrance of my (future) dorm, Dr. Jameson unlocked the door and stood aside to let us enter.

Once inside, Dr. Jameson pointed out the Resident Matron's apartment, just across the hallway from the entrance doors. She told Mom that the entrance as well as the door at the end of the hallway had buzzers that sounded in the matron's apartment if anyone went in or out.

She said that, however, the alarms were turned off during the day and evenings. Students out after curfew, though, had to buzz the dorm matron to let them in.

"Parental and special permission was required to be out after curfew, which is eight o'clock for all students on week days (Sunday evening to Thursday evening); ten o'clock for junior high students and eleven o'clock for senior high students on weekends (Friday and Saturday nights).

Dr. Jameson turned to me and said, "A word to the wise. Your dorm matron, Mrs. Finley, is very strict about school rules. She doesn't bend. It behooves you to read and 'know' your student handbook to stay out of trouble."

Right next to the Matron's apartment, there was also a big study hall. It had a number of library type tables and reference books like dictionaries and a set of encyclopedias. AND I was happy to see, soda and snack vending machines!

"Do you mind if I look around?" I asked Dr. Jameson.

"No, not at all," Dr. Jameson answered with a droll grin.

"And, ah, Mom. Can I have a couple of nickels and a penny?" I continued hesitantly.

Dr. Jameson chuckled and said, "That won't work for these vending machines. The cokes went up in price again. They now cost a dime instead of six cents. And the snacks also cost a dime."

'Merde!' I thought, but of course, didn't say out loud.

"No, Honey," Mom told me. "You can wait for dinner. We'll eat as soon as we get back home."

"Please, Mom."

"No, Jenny. You can wait," Mom cut me off.

Dr. Jameson's grin turned wryer, but she commiserated with me, "That's Mrs. Finley's rule too. She won't let you use the machines until after dinner."

"What about during the day?"

"Not then either, but you can buy snacks at the school commissary during the day except a meal times. Scholarship students man it during their free periods."

Dr. Jameson didn't pick on the irony of using the verb 'man' for girl clerks. At least she didn't seem to.

"Can I at least see what snacks they sell?" I asked Mom.

"If it's okay with Dr. Jameson, okay. But make it snappy."

"Go ahead Jenny. I'm not in a particular hurry," Dr. Jameson told me.

I think the words 'particular hurry' meant I shouldn't dawdle, so to use Mom's phrase, I 'made it snappy!').

I saw the 'Coke machine' had several other bottled drinks

besides Coca-Colas, including Moxie (wintergreen and licorice flavored soda! Yuck!). And for a dime and not six cents!

The 'snacks' tended to be the more 'nutritious' ones, like Tom's Toasted Peanuts, Ritz crackers with peanut butter, M and M's with peanuts, Reese's Cup (chocolate covered peanut butter), Sky Bars (peanut whip filling), Pay Days (peanut covered caramel), Cracker Jacks (peanuts and caramel popcorn), Almond Joys (at least they didn't have peanuts), Cheezies, Frito Corn Chips and Sun Maid Raisins. (That was a lot of peanuts and no Twinkies or Hostess Coconut Covered Snowballs!).

When I returned from my 'perusal' of the snack offerings, Dr. still was wearing her wry grin, but she immediately launched into explaining the layout of the dorm.

All of the ground floor rooms were for third years. The first and second year students' quads are all on the second floor. The fourth through seventh years (high school students) were in the other dorm, Maria Mitchel Hall, to the north of the main building.

Dr. Jameson directed us up a staircase and to my quad which was the last one on the left at the east end of the building.

All the dorm walls were ecru colored (plaster over lathing I was sure), the door frames and doors were all stained dark brown. The floors were of oak, but were darker (because of their age. I'm sure). Which got me to wondering how old the buildings were and if the school had always been a girls' academy.

When we entered my (future) quad, I was surprised how refined it was. The common room had two Mission Arts and Crafts style settees that could maybe seat three each. There were four Gunlocke style chairs with arms and a good-sized Craftsman style table. All the furniture was made of oak.

There was also a narrow refrigerator the same dark brown color as the doors. It had a small freezer so we could keep ice cream in it. (Yeah!).

Dr. Jameson pointed out my room. It was really tiny with a single bed, a desk and chair, a combination chest-of-drawers/shelves/armoire unit. There was a full-length mirror on the back of the door, though.

In my room, the armoire had about a 2'(depth) x 4'(width) x 6' (height) space to hang clothes. The shelves were above the chest-of-drawers part. The doors of the armoire had a carved motif of vines and leaves.

All the furniture was from the beginning of the twentieth century by my estimate. Well, except for the chairs and table in the lounge. They were from the Craftsman Period a couple of decades or so later.

There were two large windows (which I would learn later were problematic for the obvious reason that they made the room colder in winter!). All the other rooms had a single window.

This was to be my world for two years, when I would move downstairs. Only after three years would I graduate to the luxury of a senior high suite with their larger bedrooms and only two students per suite and not four (or three for me this year).

After this little tour we drove back to Cambridge. Of course, it was going to be too late to shop that day. But after dinner, Mom had me start making out OUR (and not my!) long packing list of quilts, blankets and down comforters, et cetera!

I went to bed at ten o'clock, but was much too excited to go right to sleep. I just lay (intransitive) there for quite a while wondering what destiny had laid (transitive) out in front of me.

Also. I didn't know how to talk about your part in my story but in the 3rd person with you reading this. I hope that's okay.

Written the 6th to the 11th of March, 1963.

March 12, 1963

Dr. Jameson,

I don't know if you realized how stressed I was about the exam, though I guess you did, since you're a psychologist and all. I was really scared to death, due to me being an O.C.D. personality type. (Is that the right way to say that?).

Sincerely,
Jenny

Journal: Thursday, August 24th, 1961

Thursday, I began a blur of hunting through boxes, chests and steamer trunks in everyone's closets (except Mike's, of course). Mom told me I could take anything I found to decorate my room at school except for things that belonged to Karen or Mike. For those, I would need their permission.

She said I should particularly check out our attic. That I might find some interesting things there and she didn't think anything there belonged to Mike or Karen.

The closets were a bust. Boxes of books, boxes of old photos, boxes of old toys, boxes of old electronics and one in Mom's closet with her bridal bouquet and wedding dress!

I wasted the entire morning working through the closets and then Mom told me I had to put everything back where I found them!

After lunch, I was thinking about just laying around and reading, but Mom encouraged me to look through the stuff in the attic. I wasn't too thrilled about the prospect, but I went ahead.

The access to the attic was one of those pulldown ladders. It was too high for me to reach up and pull down, even with a step stool, so I had to get Mom to help me. When she pulled the down the ladder and unfolded it, dust flew everywhere. She told me not to worry about it. That I could clean the mess up later! That was something to look forward to. (Not!).

I climbed to the top of the ladder and looked around. It was too dark to really see anything but vague shapes. I called out to Mom and asked her if there was a light. She told me there was a bulb that hung down from the ceiling and it had a pull cord to turn it on.

I climbed on up, but I couldn't see the bulb. It was too dark. I took a step and then felt something in my hair. I squealed and jerked my hand to my hair to brush whatever it was off. I hit the bulb with my fingers. It had been the cord from the bulb that was in my hair. Luckily, I wasn't wearing a ring or I could have shattered the bulb and its glass could have fallen down all over me.

I pulled the cord and the light came on, but it was really

freaky. The attic looked like a scene from a Boris Karloff horror film. There were spider webs everywhere and a thick layer of dust covered everything.

There were old, dust-covered curtains covering miscellaneous chairs and odd pieces of furniture. A chenille bed spread was thrown over some rolled-up carpets. I could see that they would probably be too big for my dorm room, but I decided to take a look anyway. I flipped the chenille off of the carpets and started to unroll one when a big brown spider came crawling out of the hole at its center.

I screeched and stomped on the spider as it tried to scamper away. 'Poor thing! But it had no right to scare me like that!' I thought.

I flipped the chenille back over the carpets and leaving well enough alone. Then I flipped one of the old curtains off of what was obviously some cardboard boxes. Maybe, I was too energetic in my flipping, though, because I sent dust flying into the air. That sent me into a sneezing fit that lasted a couple of minutes. Well, maybe not that long, but it seemed like it!

When I had (mostly) gotten over my sneezes, I attacked one of the boxes. At least the tape on the box was old, so it wasn't too hard to tear off the box.

What treasure was inside? Torn, lace, window curtains; stained, crocheted doilies; an old army blanket; and a heap of old clothes. Then I tore open another box. It was filled with old pairs shoes, along with a few unmatched ones.

In the fifth box, which was long, but not too deep. I found a beautiful, little Persian carpet (It was a 'prayer rug' as I later found out in World Religions). I thought it would look good next to my bed in the dorm.

After going through several more boxes of junk, I noticed what was obviously a table lamp covered with an old curtain. Carefully, I pulled the curtain off and under it was a leaded glass lamp with a bronze base! It had a blue and green, dragonfly motif !

I just sat down on the filthily floor and started at it. Even in the dark of the attic, it glittered faint blue and green strands of light across the floor from the bare bulb hanging from the roof beams shining on it.

I cautiously picked it up and looked it over, but couldn't see any cracks in the glass or damage to its base. I needed to look it over in better light to make sure though.

So, I set it down, stood up, picked it up again and headed for the ladder. I considered how I was going to get it down the ladder and realized I would have to do it by myself. Two people would be silly for such a light lamp. What's more, they would just get in each other's way.

So, I set it down to the side of the opening for the ladder and backed down the ladder until the lamp was at my chest level. I moved my feet out until they were against the ladder rails. Then I turned my toes out and sort of under the rails to keep from falling.

Taking a deep breath, I picked up the lamp and set it on the rung right in front of me. Holding the lamp on that rung, I took a step down and placed my feet like before. Then I moved the lamp down a rung. I repeated this twelve more times until I was standing on the laundry room floor.

With sweat dripping down the sides of my face and the middle of my back, I took in a deep breath. I couldn't remember breathing the whole time I was coming down the ladder, but I must have. I couldn't have held my breath for that long. Could I?

I walked into the kitchen and carefully set the lamp on the table. Then I called out to Mom and asked her to come there.

When she walked in, she smiled and said, "It's a pretty thing isn't it? I forgot it was up in the attic."

I didn't know what to say, but when I got my wits about me, I asked what she knew about the lamp.

Mom said it was handed down to Dad by his grandfather. Excited, I said it looked a lot like the Tiffany Lamps I had seen in an exhibition at the MFA (Museum of Fine Arts). To which she said she thought Dad's father had said it was from the Tiffany Studio in New York.

I was floored and asked what it was doing gathering dust in our attic. I told Mom it could be worth a lot of money. She said Dad had never liked it, but she just couldn't force herself to give it away.

"Give it away!" I screeched. "Are you crazy? It's a

Tiffany!"

Then Mom nonchalantly asked me if I wanted it. I didn't know how to answer her. I was speechless.

When I finally found my voice again, I told her that, of course, I wanted it! Thinking about what that meant, I asked her what should I do with it, though. Where should I keep it?

Grinning, she replied that since it was a table lamp, she imagined it should be on my table. I asked her what she was talking about, that I didn't have a table.

She asked me what about my desk in my dorm room. Wasn't that a table?

"At school?" I asked her unbelievingly. "What if it got broken? Or worse, stolen?"

In response, she pointed out it had been sitting up in the attic. She told me, "Listen Jenny, you take it. You appreciate its beauty and will enjoy it."

"But Dad…" I began. Mom, however, cut me off, telling me Dad didn't like it and wouldn't care if I took it. I wasn't so sure about that, especially if he realized how much it was worth. I wasn't going to argue though!

I took it to my room, walking carefully up the stairs and looked it over. Even though it had been covered with the curtain, there was a lot of dust on it. I wasn't sure how to clean it, but I knew someone who would. Grandmother McDonald, if she was feeling well enough to talk to me.

I went to find Mom and she was still in the kitchen. I asked her if she thought Grandmother is well enough to talk to me on the telephone.

She told me she thought so. That Grandmother was getting up and around now. Anyway, she had a phone in her bedroom and could lie down and talk to me if she got too tired.

I called Grandmother up and she was in the kitchen having some tea and biscuits. She uses the British word for cookies, though I don't know why. She's thoroughly American and her family has been here since the 1870s.

We talked for quite a while about how she was doing and about me going to Willard. Mom had told her last night about my admission exam and she congratulated me.

After a while, I asked her what I should use to clean a

bronze and leaded glass lamp.

She chuckled and asked me, "You found the Tiffany, huh?"

"Grandmother!" I squealed. "You knew about it!"

"That silly son-in-law of mine has no idea what his grandfather gave him! I'm glad you found it."

I told her I was going through stuff in the attic hunting for things to decorate my room at school and I found it. Even though it was covered with an old curtain, I told her it was really dusty and needed cleaning. I asked her what I should do.

She told me it wasn't hard. That I just had to be really careful. That I should use a really soft cloth and clean all of the surfaces of the glass, inside and out with pure lemon oil and that is was okay to use the oil on the bronze base too.

She told me she had some oil that I could use. Also, that I had to be sure to get all the oil off when I was finishing up, so it wouldn't get gummy. That would make the next cleaning really difficult.

Then she suggested I get Karen or Mom to bring me over the next day and we could clean it together!

"Would you Grandmother? I mean are you… feeling well enough?"

She answered that she was quite well enough to sit at a table and clean a lamp with her favorite granddaughter! Then she told me to call Mom to the phone so she could talk to her.

So, I called Mom and she talked to Grandmother about it. Mom wasn't altogether sure, but Grandmother talked her into it and asked Mom to bring me over at ten the next day.

Grandmother also wanted me to stay for lunch and have soup and sandwiches with her. To cut off any worries, she told Mom the day nurse would help her prepare everything.

When Mom and Grandmother finished their call, I started to head up to my bedroom, but Mom asked me where did I think I was going.

That meant she had something in mind for me that I probably wasn't going to like. So I replied that I didn't know. That I was thinking about doing some reading. I told her it was for school. In reality, I had in mind to definitely and finally finish up 'Wuthering Heights.' I only lacked about twenty pages.

Unimpressed, she asked me could I do something for her first. That was like handing someone a signed check that wasn't filled out, but what can you say when it's your mother?

"Yeah?" I asked. Not really saying yes. More like asking 'What?'

She told me I had left the laundry room in quite a mess, so I needed to sweep the room all out. Then clean off all the shelves and the washer and dryer with some dish detergent and hot water. Then to finally mop the floor. Also, that I should make sure the laundry baskets were clean and didn't have any dust left on them.

Like I said, she had something in mind I wasn't going to like!

I smiled and said, "Sure Mom." Reminding myself I had just been given a Tiffany Lamp worth no telling how much.

I only took a break to eat supper and by the time I was finished, it was time to take a bath and get ready for bed. Karen was out on a date, though, and I didn't know when Dad would be getting home, so I was feeling anxious about a bath.

I really wanted a good soak after all the grungy work I had done, but instead, I took a quick hot shower. Even if Mom was at home and Dad would be unlikely to try anything, I felt really ill-at-ease.

I was in both a good mood and a bad mood when I crawled into bed. I was happy about the lamp, but mad because I didn't get to take a good, long soak!

Written the 13th to the 18th of March, 1963.

March 18th, 1963

Dr. Jameson,

Mrs. Finley came to wake me up at two o'clock this morning. Mom called to tell me Grandpa Roberts has died. He had arteriosclerosis. I don't know if I told you that.

I just noticed I typed March 18th and it's now 3 o'clock in the morning, the 19th, but I'm too tired to correct my mistake. Mrs. Finley also woke up Sarah and Emalie when she woke me. They stayed up with me for a while, but then went back to their beds. I'm writing this letter because I have to do something and I can't sleep.

Mom said that Granny Lamont is pretty devastated. So, she's flying to Nashville to help Aunt May get ready for the funeral. Karen, Mike and I, however, won't be going with her.

It was weird that Aunt May waited an entire day to call us, but I guess with all she has to do, she forgot. Marty too. I'll have to talk to him about that. I'm upset.

I have mixed feelings about not going to the funeral. I'd like to go to be able to go and see Marty, but that's not a good reason to go right now.

Marty was planning to come see me Easter Break to stay with us and get set up for the fall, he was accepted to Harvard conditionally. He told me Sunday afternoon on a phone call. So, Grandpa Roberts had to have died after that. He would have surely told me otherwise.

Marty can't call me often because Aunt May won't let him. But that's another story.

I'll talk to you about everything today at my session at noon. I don't know if I should go to class. I can't think, so it would be pretty useless.

I'll leave this letter at the office and ask the secretary to give it to you. But I can't talk to you… or anyone right now. I would break down and I don't want to do that where everyone would be looking at me.

Yours truly, *Jenny*

P.S. Maybe, I think I'll just stay in my room and write about Friday, August 25th, 1961.

Journal: Friday, August 25th, 1961

In spite of my mixed moods the night before (Thursday, the 24th), I woke up feeling a little better. That feeling disappeared, though, when I walked into the kitchen. Dad was sitting at the table, leaning back in his chair and sipping his coffee.

I wanted to turn around and walk, no run, back upstairs to my room, but I was hungry and wanted to eat breakfast. Undecided, I stood stock still in the hallway, just outside the kitchen door unsure of what to do.

Dad turned around towards me and sort of smirked. At least I think it was a smirk. With Dad, I'm not sure how much my emotions distort my perception. Maybe he's not as disgusting as I see him. I just knew I was on edge whenever he was around.

After dawdling a moment and finishing his coffee, he sat his cup on the table, leaned over and kissed Mom on the cheek. Then he stood up and told Mom, "Well, I guess I'd better head for the office. I need to go over the syllabi for my classes again. They'll be starting soon."

Then he headed straight for me. I thought he was going to try something on me in guise of a hug, so I dodged to the side. He just walked out of the kitchen past me. Then he headed towards the front door, only pausing to pick up his attaché case from the hallway side table before walking out the door.

Mom stood up and saw me. I don't think she had been aware I was just outside the kitchen. With a smile, she greeted me, "Oh. Hi, Honey! I didn't know you were there. I was about to go wake you up to come eat. We need to head out in about thirty minutes to go over to Mother's. What would you like to eat?"

Relaxing a little, I smiled at her and told her I was pretty hungry and asked her if she could fix me some French toast and bacon.

She grinned and said, "You are hungry then. Sure, I'll fix some up for you. How many pieces?"

"Three?" I asked hesitantly.

"I guess you worked up quite an appetite yesterday," she chuckled.

"Yeah, I guess so," I replied.

Then she told me to go ahead and get some juice and milk. That she would have my food ready in a couple of minutes.

"Thanks, Mom," I said as I got two glasses out of the cupboard and poured myself some milk and orange juice.

After breakfast, we headed straight over to Grandmother's. Mom just dropped me off at the curb and told me to tell Grandma she'd visit for a while when she came to pick me up after lunch.

I carefully laid the lamp on the car seat, got out of the station wagon and then picked up the lamp again. I'd held it in my lap all the way from home.

When I started to close the car door bumping my rear against it, but Mom called out to not worry about closing the door. That she would get it. Then she slid over and grabbed the door handle and pulled the door shut with a soft thump.

I started up the walk, but then looked over my shoulder and yelled, "Thanks for the ride, Mom. I'll see you after lunch."

As I was walking up the steps to Grandmother's porch, she opened her door and then her screen door and shouted, "How's my favorite granddaughter?"

I laughed and said that I bet she told that to all her granddaughters!

With a mischievous grin, she admitted that, truthfully, she did. However, she continued by telling me that I was special, though.

She gave me a peck on the cheek as I walked in and as she closed the door, she told me to go on in the dining room. That all the cleaning supplies were already there.

I was surprised to see a sheet of plastic spread over the top of Grandma's huge dining table. She had a neat pile of cloths, a bottle of 'Everclear' (190 proof alcohol = 95% alcohol content!) and a bottle labeled 'Olio di Limone Italiano.'

I asked what all this was about and, without blinking, she replied it was what I needed to clean the lamp. Suspicious that she had been overdoing it, I asked her, "And you just happened to have all this stuff just lying around the house?"

She laughed and told me that actually she did, except for the plastic sheet.

Hearing my skepticism, she explained that she had bought the lemon oil at the local pharmacy and kept it around to make up cleaning products.

I asked her what about the 'Everclear' and she said she bought it at the liquor store.

I laughed and asked her was it for cleaning products too.

It was her turn to laugh. But she answered, "Actually, yes. I use it to clean delicate things, like jewelry and watches. You know that lots of things that have metals in them corrode or get gummed up with detergents and petroleum products. Even the so called 'gentle' dishwashing detergents have salts in them that can attack metals."

"Gold?" I asked and she responded, "Not pure gold, of course., but most jewelry isn't made with 24 carat gold. Most are a gold alloy. No use in taking chances with heirlooms!"

I blinked at that and wondered what heirloom jewelry she owned.

Dropping that discussion, I asked her what about the 'Olio di Limone Italiano.'

She explained that the Italian oil was pure expressed lemon oil, whereas the so-called lemon oil furniture polishes made in America all were diluted with kerosene. ('Probably not kerosene,' I thought, 'but most likely petroleum distillates').

I asked her how did she know all that (about the lemon oil) and she responded that she had asked an antique restorer who had a shop in the Cambridge Antique Market. He had told her what he used.

Grinning, she admitted, "He might have been prejudiced, though, since he was Italian!"

"And where did you get the plastic sheeting?" I asked.

"Oh, there's this nice painter. You know, a house painter, not an artist, who goes to my church. Well, yesterday after I talked to you, I gave him a call and asked him how I could set up a place to work in the house. I think you call it 'un atelier.' You know a workshop for us to work together cleaning the lamp."

When she explained she would be using lemon oil, he told her she needed some plastic sheeting and he would bring over that morning. He had told her it was too small to use for his work. She suspected, though, he wasn't altogether truthful about that.

He just warned her to be careful about the vapors. (I doubted she told him about the 'Everclear'!). When he came over and saw where we would be working, though, he said since it was such a big room and we'd only be using a small amount of oil, we should be alright. A fan wouldn't be 'amiss,' though, he told her.

"And the cloths?" I asked.

She smiled wistfully and told me they were old tee shirts of my Grandfather's. She said she had always used them for dusting and waxing her furniture. She said they didn't leave lint like terrycloth or other kinds of cloth do. She considered them an inexpensive substitute for 'un chamois.'

She told me that when Grandfather died, she gave all his clothes to charity. But she kept his tee shirts and cut them up to use on things she didn't want to leave lint on.

Impressed, I told her that she was amazing!

She just chuckled and said, "You learn a few tricks if you live to be eighty-three!"

With that we started cleaning the Tiffany Lamp. Of course, we had to take the glass part off of the bronze base to start cleaning the glass, but we had fun working together.

Starting by dusting off the glass with feather duster (that I hadn't noticed on the buffet), we went on to wipe of the glass using the 'Everclear.' Which actually made me a little lightheaded, until Grandmother noticed and turned on the fan.

"Do people actually drink this stuff?" I asked.

Her reply was short and to the point, "Only fools."

Then we cleaned and polished, cleaned and polished, and cleaned and polished the glass inside and out, using the lemon oil. Three times!

Then we cleaned off the residue of the lemon oil with more 'Everclear,' before we polished the bronze base (twice!). But when we didn't clean the lemon oil off of it, I asked Grandmother why and she explained that the oil would protect the bronze from tarnishing where it was touched! (How do I carry it or even turn it on then?).

When we had started on the base, I saw the power cord was

cracked, so I was going to have to go by the hardware store to buy a new cord and a better plug-in before I could see what it looked like with the bulb turned on.

Grandmother, however, turned on the chandelier over the dining table and the glass sent ribbons of blue and green light onto the table.

She also said I should get a real antique restorer like the Italian guy (artisan, in her words) to replace the wiring. "To maintain its historic value," she explained.

When I said I couldn't afford that, she said she'd pay for it as one of my Christmas presents. ('But Christmas is months away,' I thought guiltily).

Anyway, by the time we finished up, Grandmother was pretty tired and went to rest on her bed. I hoped she hadn't overdone it. But I cleaned up all the mess and headed out to toss the rags and the plastic tarp in the (trash) barrel.

As I was tossing the debris in the barrel, a car pulled up to the curb. An older woman with grey streaked red hair stepped out. She was wearing something like a traditional nurse's uniform (of the white short-sleeved dress type). Everything except the starched, white nursing cap.

She walked up to me smiling and said I must be Jenny. Sticking her hand out to shake, she told me she was Nurse O'Connor, but I should call her Nora. She spoke English with a beautiful Irish brogue.

[As I started to write out this conversation with Nurse Nora, I wasn't sure about including it. But I had gone to the Boston Central Library at Copley Square on Saturday and spent the whole day there studying Tomas De Bhaldraithe's 'English to Irish Dictionary' [1959] and Patrick Stephen Dinneen's 'Gaedilge agus Béarla' (An Irish to English Dictionary) [1904], to get the spellings of Nurse Nora's Irish words.

Not an easy task! The words were quite different from Scots and not pronounced at all like they're spelled! (A lot like French words, not phonetic at all and with lots of letters not pronounced!). On top of that, the two dictionaries spelled the same word differently! The De Bhaldraithe's used the modern spellings from the Irish government's language reforms, while

Dinnen's predated them by fifty years. For Nurse Nora's English, I've written it out like it sounded to me!]

Jovially, Nurse Nora told me, "Yer nanna ken be a handful! She told me ta 'nay' come afore noon today, but to please get 'er messages' fer 'er. She wanted ta spend time alone wit' ya, but needed somethin' ta fix fer lunch fer ya two!"

I admitted to her that I wondered why she wasn't there when I arrived.

"Ay would a been, but she's been doin' so much bettah. Ay thought she'd do fine fer a few hours," she explained.

"Well, you go on in and give her her messages," I told her.

Nurse O'Connor burst out laughing. "Ay been wit' m'athair and 'e only speaks Irish at home. It takes me a bit to change ta English. But 'messages' means shoppin' now a days in Ireland."

"Your mother, he?" I asked and she laughed even harder. "M'athair means 'my father' an' 'máthair' means mother."

I laughed with her and told her I could speak a little Scots, but I guessed not Irish Gaelic.

"That's 'Teanga Ghaelach' in Irish," she told me.

"'Teanga Glaelach must mean 'Gaelic Tongue?'" I asked.

"Y'er a cailín cliste!" she chuckled.

"I know 'cailín' (pronounced Colleen!). It means girl. But 'cliste?'" I asked her.

"It means smaat."

"Thank you, Nurse O'Connor."

"That's Nora!"

"Thanks, Nurse Nora. I'll take the 'messages' to the kitchen. Why don't you go on in and check on Grandmother?"

"She's doin' okay?" she asked.

I told her she was fine, but near the end of cleaning my lamp she did tire out. That she went and laid down about thirty minutes before.

"If ya ken take tha 'messages' in, I'll go check on 'er. They're in the back seat an' the car's unlocked," Nurse Nora said indicating the groceries.

She went on in to check on Grandmother and I grabbed the two bags groceries and took them to the kitchen. (They weren't that heavy). I had arranged the food in the cupboards and fridge and started making some grilled cheese sandwiches for everyone when Nurse Nora finally came to the kitchen.

"That's a pretty thing," she said indicating the Tiffany Lamp, which I had placed on the kitchen table. "That's what ya worked on?"

"Yes, it is, but I'd better put on the counter."

"Ay'll do it fer ye. Just keep on wit' tha sandwiches," she said, carefully moving the lamp.

"Oh, I see ya left out tha tin of tomato soup. Ay'll make that up, put it on the stove an' also heat some water ta 'wet the tae.'"

"I bet 'wet the tae' means pouring boiling water over the tea."

"Tá tú cliste…"

I broke in, "'Tu' probably means 'you' and 'cliste' means 'smart.' So 'tá' means 'are?'"

"Close, but 'tá' by itself means 'yes,' but 'tá tú' means 'you are.'"

"So, you said, 'I'm smart'?"

"No, that's 'Táim cliste."

I was confused for a second. Then I got it! "You're teasing me! 'Táim' means 'I am' and 'Tá tú' means 'you are!'"

Nurse Nora laughed and it was a nice sound. Then she said, "Like Ay said afore, 'Tá tú cailín cliste!'"

"Taing do!"

"That has to be 'thank you' in Scots."

"Tha sin ceart!"

"That's almost like Irish. 'Sin céart' means 'That's right.' Enough school lessons in Irish, though! And Scots, too, fer that mattah!" she said chuckling.

We worked 'companionably' preparing lunch. When the grilled cheeses were ready, Nurse Nora said, "Ay think tha soup is ready. If you ken put tha grilled cheese sandwiches on some plates an' 'wet tha tae.' Ay'm sure ya know where tha taepot is. Ay'll go get yer Nanna."

The three of us (including Grandmother) carried on a lively conservation. Nurse Nora told us some wild stories about her working as a visiting, public health nurse in 'Southie' (a working-class Irish neighborhood in South Boston).

I noticed she was wearing a purple shield pin with Y.S.N. across the top and 'Lux et Veritas' as its moto on one collar and on the other was a gold Sigma Theta Tau key with diamonds (?) and amethyst around its border.

I asked her what they were and she told me the purple shield was for her nursing degree that she got at the Yale School of Nursing in 1933. The Sigma Theta Tau was the academic honor society for nursing. She just sort of tossed those two bits of information out there as if they were of no importance, but you could have knocked me over with a feather!

She went right on telling us about her work without pausing. Her first position was as a Registered Nurse at New Haven Hospital in Connecticut, where she worked for a couple of years. Then she became a nurse-midwife and worked in 'Southie' from 1936 to 1957.

She said she was getting too old for that kind of work, up and down five stories of staircases. So, in 1955, when they started bulldozing the buildings in the New York Streets District for the 'housing projects,' she became an obstetrics nurse at the Boston University School of Medicine.

Then this year, at the ripe old age of fifty-six, she went back to being a visiting nurse, because as she expressed it, "Ay like workin' where Ay'm closer ta ma patients then Ay ken bae in hospital."

As we finished our lunch, Mom came to get me.

Right off, Grandmother started in on that she was doing so well she didn't need, "Round the clock baby-sitting anymore," to use her words.

Mom came back with, "Now Mother…" and they started arguing about it. I had the feeling that this happened pretty often. But Nurse Nora gently inserted herself into the argument and calmed everything 'down a notch.'

It was obvious that she was an old hand at handling cantankerous patients and finally got Grandmother to agree to, "givin' it a tray fer one mare week."

On the way home, Mom told me they had had the same 'discussion' (meaning argument) since we had returned from the reunion and she started spending her evenings with

Grandmother.

When we got home, Mom set me to going through all of my clothes to see what I needed to get for school. It took me all afternoon since I had to pretty much had to try on everything to sort out 'too small' from 'sort of fits' from 'not warm enough for fall and winter' from 'I don't like it anymore!'

By the time for dinner, I was down to:
1. Four pairs of jeans;
2. Two pairs of slacks (which, to be truthful, were a little tight);
3. The new, boy's white dress shirt;
4. The dingy, white, ruffled, short-sleeved blouse (which, of course, Mom tossed out as soon as she saw it);
5. A bunch of tee shirts (some of which were getting a little tight too);
6. A single polo shirt (the blue one);
7. A Henley (a heavy, long sleeved sort of tee shirt) passed down from Mike, which unfortunately fit fine and looked okay (to Mom!), though it was several years old;
8. Three wool sweaters (which fit okay, but five were too small!);
9. My pretty, green trapeze dress;
10. A number of pairs of wool, Norwegian knee socks (too many!);
11. My new lingerie;
12. Two pairs of nylons;
13. My garter belt;
14. Two pairs of Mary Janes (black and cordovan);
15. One pair of tennis shoes (sneakers);
16. Winter boots (felt-lined Sorels) which I could still wear if I used thin socks;
17. My school uniform kilt (which would make five with four others on order);
18. My blue blazer (making four with the two uniform blazers and tweed one on order).

That was all as far as clothes were involved! I saw I was going to have to spend a lot of time shopping before I was ready for school (in eight days!).

Then I had this awful thought. Either Mom or even worse, Karen, would probably be taking me shopping!

Mom came up to see how it was going and to tell me dinner was ready. She looked at the clothes piled on my bed and the much bigger pile of discards on the floor with a 'jaundiced' eye. (That's non-literal, Marty!).

"You've only got one skirt?" she asked.

"I only had three besides the uniform skirt for school we bought for the test day," I replied. "And those three are too short to be decent," I went on. (How come I kept getting taller without getting anything in the breast department?).

"Put on one so I can see it," Mom instructed.

I did and had a lot of trouble zipping it up. I had only considered the length, but it seemed that maybe my hips were getting wider too! (Along with my waist, so still no curves!).

"Yep," she said, "Definitely too small and too short."

"I really don't need a bunch of skirts, though," I said. "I'll have the uniform ones and can wear jeans when I'm not in class."

"I don't think so," Mom told me.

"What do you mean?" I asked.

Mom sighed and told me, "I talked to Emalie's Mom and she said that students have to wear skirts whenever you're off the school grounds, as well as… well, the uniforms to class."

"What?" I screeched.

"It's in the student's handbook. You can only wear slacks when heading home with your parents on weekends."

"You're kidding. Right?"

"Nope. Not at all."

"What about when it's snowing?"

"Wool stockings, wool tights, but nylons when it's not too cold. It might be good to get you some over-the-calf boots, like some riding boots. Maybe a long coat that goes down to your calfs too."

I dropped onto my bed and laid back on it, my hands holding my head. "Mom!"

"Don't be such a drama queen! All the girls will have the same rules. Oh, and the hems of the skirts can't be higher than two inches above the knee."

116

"It just gets better and better!" I grouched sarcastically.

Mom walked over to my closet and frowned. "Do all of these tee shirts still fit? Several are pretty faded and worn."

I fibbed and told her they were still okay. She turned around and looked at me doubtfully. Then she reached for one of the dingier, worn and too-small ones, took it off its hanger and handed it to me. "Here. Try this on and let me see."

"Well, that one is maybe a little small," I admitted.

She tossed it in the Good Will pile and started taking all 'ses semblables' (similar ones) off their hangers and adding them to the Good Will pile.

"Mom!" I yelped, "Those are still fine!"

"Want to try them on and show me?"

"No," I grumbled.

"Look, Jenny, if you had a younger sister you could hand them down. But you don't, so it's better to let some other girl enjoy them."

"I could hand them down to my daughters," I muttered.

Mom raised her eyebrows and asked, "Really? In twenty years?"

With that Mom left and a couple of minutes later yelled at me to get myself down to dinner.

After diner, I went up to my room and started folding up the clothes in the Good Will pile and bagging them. When I finished, I sat down on my bed, brooded and felt sorry for myself.

But then I started reading 'Nicholas Nickleby' by Dickens. That didn't help my mood at all. I had visions of Willard being as awful as Dicken's notorious Yorkshire public school, Dotheboys Hall! (In England, a 'public school' is the same thing as a 'private school' in America).

Anyway, though I was really tired, I wasn't sleepy at all, so I read on 'til about three in the morning.

When I finally fell asleep, I had nightmares about being caned (beaten with a rattan cane, British school punishment) like the poor, abused Smike in the book. Just for wearing jeans in the dorm! Needless to say, I passed a restless night!

Written the week of the 20th to the 25th of March, 1963.

Sunday, March 25th, 1963

Dear Dr. Jameson,

I started writing the account about August 25 last Tuesday morning, even before our session. I'm glad I could see you at noon and I'm sorry about all my blubbering. I felt better after the cry, even if I don't really remember what I said or worse, what you said.

Sorry!

We'll have to talk about August the 25th of last year again. I don't know if we talked about it last Tuesday or not. I'm really going psycho or having early onset Alzheimer's.

Also, Marty can't come during Easter break. Aunt May threw a fit and yelled at him. In front of all the relatives and guests at the funeral parlor during the viewing. (I'm glad I didn't go to the funeral. I've never seen a dead person and I would have been expected to 'view' Grandpa).

About Aunt May's fit. She said Marty was being ungrateful in abandoning her to go to Harvard right after her father died. That he should just stay in Nashville like 'a good son would.'

I want to talk about that. Maybe we can talk about that before we talk about August 25th, at my session, next week.

Sincerely yours, Jenny

P.S. Sorry about the Gaelic! Marty is a bad influence on me. Sometimes I feel like I'm in a competition with him linguistically. Not really. I'm just joking!

Again, this a long account about things not connected to the situation with Dad. Just what happened.

Journal: Saturday, August 26th to Saturday, September 2nd, 1961

That Saturday, Mom let me sleep in 'til noon, but after dragging me from my comfortable bed and force-feeding me brunch (too late for breakfast), then she headed out shopping with me in tow.

I didn't think I needed that much (foolish me!), but over that next week to the next Saturday, Mom and I or Karen and I (on two days), shopped at Fillene's, Gilchrist's, Harvard Coop, Jordan Marsh's, Kennedy's, Sears and Stearn's. (That's in alphabetical order, not the order we attacked them!). Oh yes, and of course, Mrs. McCaffrey's for my uniforms and Mrs. Reynolds for my lingerie.

We shopped every day except for Sunday and not then only because stores were all closed. Blue Laws!

After all these expeditions, I ended up with:
1. Three more pairs of wool 'dress' slacks;
2. Five more skirts (besides the ones Mrs. McCaffrey was already making for me! Sigh!);
3. Four more dresses (three which were shirt-dresses);
4. Seven more blouses, four long-sleeved and three short-sleeved. This doesn't count Mrs. McCaffrey's;
5. Four more sweaters;
6. Two sweater-vests (I didn't have any before);
7. The grey tweed blazer with leather elbow patches;
8. Two pairs of over-the-calf boots (one cordovan and one black);
9. Five pairs of pumps of various colors and heel heights including one pair in green (like my eyes) and one pair of what the English would call 'court shoes' in black. (All the shoes had 'kitten heels' except one dressy cordovan pair, which had three-inch heels. Well, two pair counting the green ones, which also had three-inch heels);
10. Another pair of tennis shoes (sneakers);
11. Five pairs of tights (in different weights of wool) and two more pairs of nylons;

12. Three winter coats: one a mid-length in a bouclé wool fabric; one a maxi-length (to the middle of the calf) waxed Mackintosh; and a mid-length, brown colored, sheared, beaver fur coat with a red fox collar and cuffs! (Karen chose that one and charged it to Dad's American Express Card. At least the coat was on sale at 30% off. Sigh…);
13. A 'bunch of makeup,' toiletries, perfumes and a case to put them in (of course, bought on one of Karen's days);
14. Plush Egyptian cotton towels, washcloths and bathrobe;
15. A shower caddy and flip flops;
16. Orders for three sets of ballet exercise wear (two black, long-sleeved, leotards with matching mini wrap skirts. Two pair of transition tights and two regular ones in ballet pink; and two pairs of soft leather 'chaussons de ballet' in ballet pink. No 'pointe' shoes required. Yet! (I don't see myself needing them any time soon. Like ever!).

About this: I had gotten a letter from Madame Roget, my future ballet teacher, on Monday, the 27th. She wrote I would need a navy blue, long sleeved, bodysuit. Really a long-sleeved leotard with legs! Mrs. Reynolds's was designated as the shop to get it made at. Madame Roget apologized for the late date at notifying me, as if it was her fault, I applied so late.

How she knew to get in touch with me, I don't know. Did Dr. Jameson say something? I'm not accusing or anything, but what if I had decided to make the long bus trip(s) to be on the swim team at the Lynch/van Otterloo YMCA. I'm just saying).

Anyway, going on:

17. A new down duvet and pillow and three sheet sets (the only things we bought at Sears);
18. A Japanese Cherry Blossom Print (Sakura) duvet cover with a matching pillowcase (from Fillene's);
19. A pair of 'fuzzy' bedroom slippers with bunny ears. (What can I say? They were cute!);

20. Heavy lace curtains (Probably a big mistake, since although they would make my room nice and sunny, they would do nothing to keep the cold out. They were pretty, though, with a sort of double wedding ring pattern. Too bad I didn't have a twin bed size quilt with the same pattern. The one Grandmother made for me was for a full-sized bed. Sigh…);

21. All my school supplies (including two slide rules! One with trig scales and the other logarithms) from the Coop using Dad's membership and his American Express Card;

22. A leather messenger bag (by Mark Cross!).

On Wednesday, the thirtieth, (one of Karen's days), we went up to Marblehead to Mrs. McCaffrey's to get my school uniforms and I had a surprise waiting for me.

When we walked in her shop, there was this gorgeous, green velvet, floor-length gown hanging on display behind the counter. It had a round neckline with an illusion sweetheart shape. Its flutter sleeves gave the appearance of a delicate cape. Its overlay, though, was what made it so striking. It was of sheer chiffon with exquisitely textured embroidery in a maple leaf motif.

Mrs. McCaffrey, alerted to our presence by the jingling bell of the entry door, ducked into the shop from the work room in the back of store. Seeing it was Karen and me, she broke into a big smile and greeted us, "Guid moirne lassies! Whit like are ye?" (Good morning girls. How are you?)

"Och! 'm daein fine. Whit aboot yerself?" (Oh, I'm doing fine. How about you?) I answered.

"Meickle guid" (Really well) she replied. Then smiling at me eyeing the gown, she asked, "D'ye like it?" (Do you like it?) pointing at the gown.

"Och aye! Ay pure like it! Iz wall lookit!" (Oh yes! I really like it! It's beautiful!).

"A kennt ye waud," she said with a chuckle. "D'ye wint tae try't on?" (Do you want to try it on?)

"Ay dinnae ken. Maist Ay?" (I don't know. May I?) I replied.

"Whyfore nocht? Iz yer awn!" (Why not? It's yours).

"Mine! I mean, My awn?"

"Yer sister dinnae tell ye?" (Your sister didn't tell you?) she asked as she looked towards Karen.

"I think Mrs. McCaffey just asked if you knew about your gown," Karen said with a smirk.

Ignoring Karen, I answered Mrs. McCaffrey, "Nae, she dinnae." (No, she didn't).

She reached up and took the gown down of the clothing hook and turned towards me, "Och! Haur ye gae. Try't on!" (Well, here, [take it] and try it on).

I turned to Karen and she nodded her head to the side, towards Mrs. McCaffrey and told me, "Well, go ahead!"

"Quae tae tha wark roume. A ken ye'll need a hand tae claithe yerself." (Come along to the workroom. I think you'll need help to get dressed).

"Aye. Thank ye uncolie!" (Yes. Thanks ever so much!) I said and followed her into her workroom. She opened the door for me and entered after me, closing the door behind her. (I was glad she didn't give Karen the chance to barge in!).

Anyway, the room was amazing. It was gigantic with two large tables with cuddy hole shelves under them. The cuddy holes were filled with an unbelievable number of bolts of cloth in every color, pattern and type of fabric imaginable. One whole wall was covered with cuddy hole shelves too, each cuddy hole there with its own bolts of cloth or many big spools of thread.

I'm pretty sure all the tables and furniture (a big roll-top desk and two rolling banker's chairs included) were of oak, though the measuring table tops were Formica. The two big ones had half inch grids, inch and centimeter rulers (along the sides) and single 60° and 45° vectors (from side to side) painted on them in fine lines and slender numbers.

Around the walls were five different kinds of industrial sewing machines with their own tables (which unlike the furniture) had metal supports. Three of the machines looked quite used (even antique) and the other two were obviously pretty new to judge by their paint, style and condition. Two of the machines were Berninas (one old and one new). The others were Singers (two old and one new).

Mrs. McCaffrey laid the gown on top of a big table (the one without stacks of school uniform skirts and blouses on it).

She turned to me and said, "Why dinna ye strip an A'll gae ye a hand tae claithe yerself?"

I was pretty sure 'strip' meant to 'get undressed' and not today's (American) meaning, so I took off my skirt (a new one we had bought the Monday before) and my blouse. I hadn't worn a slip since I thought I would be trying on things (including slacks) and it would just get in the way and be a pain. That left me standing there in my chemise and panties (or knickers as the Brits and probably the Scots too would call them).

Other than a very slightly raising her left eyebrow for a second, Mrs. McCaffrey appeared nonchalant about my attire or lack thereof. She picked up my gown, unhooked and unzipped it and then held it up for me to step into and slip my arms in the sleeves.

Stepping around behind me, she told me, "Haud up yer herr sae A kan dae ye up." (Hold up your hair so I can do you up). I did and she did.

Her hands on my shoulders, she turned me towards the dressing mirror in the corner and said, "Tak a guid leuk at yerself." (Take a good look at yourself).

I walked around the cutting table and over to the triple mirror. Turning this way and that, I looked at myself in amazement. In the gown I looked, dare I say, beautiful. I felt like crying.

Mrs. McCaffrey walked up behind me, put her hands on my shoulders again, turned me to face the middle mirror and told me, "Yer a meikle bonnie lassie. Mind ye o' this in tyme coming. Whane'er ye fash yerself an' think ye bina pritty, mind yerself o' whan ye first seed yerself in this gown." (You're a very pretty girl. Remember this in the future. When you fret and think you're not good looking, remind yourself of when you first saw yourself in this gown).

I turned around, hugged Mrs. McCaffrey and told her, "Thank ye uncolie, Mrs. McCaffrey! Fer this an' a'thing!" (Thank you ever so much, Mrs. McCaffrey! For this and everything!).

"Yer welcome," Mrs. McCaffrey replied as she hugged me back. Then stepping back from me, she told me, "Noo, gae me a

wee peck on ma chowk an' gae shaw yer sister yer gown."
(Now, give me peck (kiss) on my cheek and go show your sister
your gown).

I twirled around and headed out of the workshop.

When Karen saw me, her eyes got big and then she broke
into a huge smile, "Oh Jenny! That's gorgeous! I'm glad I got
Mrs. McCaffrey to make it for you!" Then as Mrs. McCaffrey
stepped into the shop, Karen thanked her effusively, "I don't
know how to tell you how grateful I am for you making this
gown for Jenny! Thank you so very much!"

Karen walked over to Mrs. McCaffrey and stuck off her
hand to shake. She took Karen's hand both of hers and told her,
"Twas ma pleishure!" (pleasure).

"Noo, lat me gaither aw o' Jenny's things, while she shifts
'er claes." (Now, let me gather all of Jenny's things while she
changes her clothes).

I was pretty sure that Karen hadn't understood what Mrs.
McCaffrey had said, so I told her, "I'll be right back after I
change back into my skirt and blouse."

When I came back holding my gown by its hanger, Mrs.
McCaffrey was putting my skirts (kilts) in a big cardboard
clothing box. Another one sat next to it, which I supposed
already had my blouses in it.

Mrs. McCaffrey looked up and told me, "Hing yer gown on
tha heck neist ta yer coaties." (Hang your gown on the rack next
to your blazers).

After I did, I came over next to her and looked at my skirts
as she folded them into the box. The labels on the skirts caught
my eye as they were black, monogramed in blue script with my
name.

As soon as I saw them, I gasped, "Oh no!"

Karen looked over at me, concerned, and asked, "What's
the matter?"

"I need to label all my clothes that I'm taking to school."

"A makkit tha labels fer a' yer claes that A shapit an'
shewed fer ye." (I made labels for all your clothes that I
designed and sewed for you), Mrs. McCaffrey informed me.

"Ye made thaim?" (You made them?) I asked and then
answered my own question. "Wall, A 'spose ye'd a haeda'v,

sith thay'v me name on thaim." (Well, I suppose you'd have to have since they have my name on them).

"Could you make some more. I mean would it be too much trouble?" Karen asked.

"Certes, A kan mak mae. Hou mony div ye need?" (Certainly, I can make more. How many do you need?).

"How many do we need?" I translated for Karen.

"Fifty?" she replied. "How long would it take you though?" she asked Mrs. McCaffrey.

"Juist a bittie. Ane A stell, A kan mak three-fower a meenit." (Just a short while. Once I set up, I can make three or four a minute).

"After she sets up, she can make three or four a minute," I translated for Karen.

"Hou meickle waud fifty cost?" (How much would fifty cost?) I then asked.

"Naething at aw." (Nothing at all).

"Nae, we maun pey ye fer yer darg," (No, we must pay you for your work) I insisted.

"It binna meickle wark," (It's not a lot of work) she replied. "Juist aboot a quarter oor." (Just a quarter of an hour or so).

"Whit aboot yer materials?" (What about your materials?) I reminded her. "Waud a dollar pey fer thaim?" (Would a dollar pay for them?)

"An' mae an," she replied. (And more than).

"We'll pey a dollar 'an." (We'll pay a dollar then).

"Greed," (Okay) she assented. "C'mon endlin'," she said motioning for us to follow her.

We followed her back into the workshop and over to an older Singer machine. Behind it were three shelves of huge thread spools (really cones more than spools). Each shelf had twelve spools, each on its own stand. The weighted metal stands each had a wire that stuck out above it that ended in a 'V.' One thread feed through its 'V' and then to the thread guide on the machine.

Over to the side was a wooden stand with I don't know how many dowels on which were placed rolls of ribbons of all colors and all kinds of fabric.

I turned my attention back to the Singer sewing machine and asked how old it was. Mrs. McCaffrey replied, "I'v haed it fer mair 'an twenty year. Iz a guid shewin-machine fer 'broiderie, this Industr'al Irish iz." (I've had it for more than twenty years. It's a good sewing machine for embroidery, this Industrial Irish).

Then she continued, "Wall Jenny, whit colours div ye want?" (What colors do you want?).

"Kan Ay'v mair 'an wan?" (Can I have more than one?) I asked.

"Certes," she responded with a chuckle.

"Kan Ay'v fifteen in white?" (Can I have fifteen in white?)

"Reebin or thread?" she asked.

I didn't understand right off, but then I saw what she meant. "White reebin an' blue thread," (White ribbon and blue thread) I replied.

"Daurk or lichtly blue?" (Dark or light blue?)

"Kan Ay'v a mid-blue?" (Can I have a medium blue?).

She directed my attention to four shades of blue on the middle shelf. "Whit mid blue?" (Which medium blue?).

"Tha ane on tha richt. A mean tha mid richt." (The one on the right. I mean the middle right).

"This?" she asked indicating the one I meant.

"Aye," I answered.

She cut three pieces of white ribbon off their roll, each about two feet long. Then she pulled down a very elongated oval, wooden embroidery hoop off of a hook on the wall. It must have been about six by twelve inches or so. In a quick, practiced motion, she then snapped out the inner oval of the hoop, stretched a ribbon across it and snapped the hoop back together.

She laid two of the pieces of ribbon and the hoop with the third piece on the sewing table. Then she seated herself, reached to grab the medium blue thread I chose and proceeded to thread the sewing machine.

She carefully placed the embroidery hoop where she wanted it, lowered the weird little presser foot (which was shaped like a tiny donut with a toothpick stuck in it), pulled a little more thread out and was off.

In fluid movements, she moved the hoop around to embroider JennyJennyJennyJennyJennyJenny
on the ribbon. All in one line of stitching. Just pulling the ribbon sideways between each 'Jenny' so the thread was stretched with no intervening stitches to rip out. The sewing had taken all of thirty seconds.

She snipped the thread, set up the second ribbon and stitched my name six times again. Then she repeated the same process for the third ribbon.

Then I picked out the same blue thread on black ribbon for eighteen more labels. Then white thread on black ribbon for eighteen more. Then finally, white thread on a medium green ribbon for eighteen more.

She snipped off the loose threads between each 'Jenny' and then cut the labels apart. She didn't measure where to cut, but all the labels ended up exactly the same length. It was amazing!

I picked up one of the labels and was surprised at its weight as well as its suppleness, so I asked Mrs. McCaffrey what kind of fabric it was.

She told me it was a double-faced, silk satin ribbon. She also said it had a weave that didn't unravel like most satin, was washable and didn't bleed at all.

She ended up making me seventy-two in all. Still, though, she refused to take more than the dollar for all of them. The whole production had taken under thirty minutes to complete!

Soon we were headed out the door with my boxes of skirts and blouses, and my blazers and gown in their plastic garment bags (the thin plastic ones like dry cleaners use).

Next, we were headed for Mrs. Reynolds's shop to pick up the lingerie that she had made for me. As we drove over, Karen explained how she had pulled off the whole thing with the gown.

Without letting me in on it, (of course!), she had called Mrs. McCaffrey and asked her to make the gown for me. As she began her conversation, Karen realized she hadn't thought things through. Mrs. McCaffrey could understand her, but it was a one-way conversation.

Then she thought about Nurse Nora being Irish and speaking Gaelic (She didn't know that Scottish Gaelic and Irish, while both were Gaelic languages were two different languages!). Anyway, she asked Mrs. McCaffrey if she could call her back in thirty minutes or so.

To which Mrs. McCaffrey answered, "Aye. Ceart!" which Karen took (correctly) as "Yes, certainly."

Anyway, Karen went over to Grandmother's hoping that Nurse Nora would be there as it was a little after three. (Karen was pretty empty headed that day!). Luck was with her, though.

Karen had been around Nurse Nora enough that she could mostly understand her. Also, Nurse Nora was hawk-eyed observant and picked up immediately if Karen hadn't understood her. If so, she would repeat what she said in a more careful English.

To make a long story short(er), Karen got Nurse Nora to call up Mrs. McCaffrey and translate for her.

Lucky again, Nurse Nora had spent her childhood in Letterkenny in County Donegal in Northern Ireland. She told Karen that if Mrs. McCaffrey spoke Scottish Gaelic, there wouldn't be any problem since it was close to the Irish she spoke in her childhood.

So, that was how Karen was able to discuss everything about the gown with Mrs. McCaffrey.

(Through Nurse Nora), she mentioned that Mrs. Reynolds was going to make some lingerie for me and was dying the fabric to match my eyes.

Mrs. McCaffrey told her that she didn't do that (dye fabrics), but Mrs. Reynolds was an expert at it. Off hand, Karen asked if she thought Mrs. Reynolds might be able to dye some cloth to make the gown.

Anyway, Mrs. McCaffrey said she would call Mrs. Reynolds and check. Well, as it just happened, Mrs. Reynolds had just gotten the dyes from England for my lingerie, but she hadn't dyed the fabric yet. "A re'l hap" (bit of luck) as Mrs. McCaffrey would say.

In any case, Mrs. Reynolds called Karen a half hour later and told her she would be more than happy to dye the fabrics. (As it turned out, Mrs. McCaffrey and she were both long-time, good friends).

When we stopped by Mrs. Reynolds's shop later that afternoon to pick up my lingerie and asked her about the whole story, she chuckled and explained how it had come to take a lot less time than she had thought it would to get the dye.

As it turned out, she had gotten a commission for this big Christmas wedding. Mayor Collins's wife, Margret, had sent a friend her way with this huge order. Eight bridesmaids' dresses and eight matching cummerbunds and pocket handkerchiefs for the groomsmen and best man.

The friend wanted all the fabrics to match exactly, but given her choice of several different fabrics, Mrs. Reynolds saw she was going to have to do the dying herself to make sure the different fabrics matched. (I thought that would be really hard since different fabrics would dye at different rates. Mrs. Reynolds had to really know her stuff!).

Anyway, Mrs. Reynolds had to call London to place the order and then have it shipped air freight to be sure she could get everything done on time!

Since she was doing all of that, she just 'piggybacked' my dyes on that order. Luckily, she also tripled the number of little cans of dyes she would have needed to do my order.

At that point in her story, Karen interrupted her and asked how much more would we need to pay her to cover the costs. She just smiled and replied 'Nothing!'

She told us the estimate she had given us would mostly cover the cost of the dye, the shipping and the customs! (I wondered what 'mostly' meant and was pretty sure that it meant that we weren't covering Mrs. Reynolds's costs at all!).

Anyway, when Mrs. Reynolds dyed the fabrics for my lingerie, she dyed the silk chiffon, charmeuse and velvet for Mrs. McCaffrey, too.

Mrs. Reynolds said she had ordered the extra dye because she liked the color, but also just on the chance I might want some more lingerie that color.

I asked Mrs. Reynolds if she had dyed the embroidered chiffon for Mrs. McCaffrey too and she replied that she had dyed the chiffon, but it wasn't embroidered when she did. She told us Mrs. McCaffrey had embroidered the chiffon herself!

(Gasp!). She went on to say that Mrs. McCaffrey was well known for her embroidery work.

Mrs. Reynolds admitted that she sometimes felt guilty for accepting some commissions, recognizing that her use of 'allover' machine woven fabric was nowhere near the artistry of Mrs. McCaffrey's unique, one-of-a-kind embroideries.

When Karen and I walked out of Mrs. Reynolds's shop, my admiration and respect for Mrs. McCaffrey had risen to a whole new level (from the high regard I already held her in). As well as for Mrs. Reynolds!

I remembered that when I first saw the gown, I had wondered where she had gotten ahold of the embroidered chiffon for the overdress. Only to then find out she, herself, had not only made the appliques, but also had machine embroidered the lace by hand! Amazing!

As Karen and I were driving back home, I started worrying about how much trouble everybody had gone to (and how much everything had cost).

When I asked Karen admitted that she suspected that both Mrs. McCaffrey and Mrs. Reynolds had put a lot more work into the dress than what they were paid for.

I pressed Karen on exactly how much my gown had cost, she smirked and told me to not worry about it. That Dad had picked up the tab, though he didn't know that yet!

That Wednesday evening and each evening the following three days were spent sewing the monogramed labels Mrs. McCaffrey had made on the clothes Mom and I or Karen and I had purchased.

I wanted to put one on my messenger bag (on the inside, of course!), but couldn't figure out a way to do it (the bag was made of really heavy leather and was unlined).

Some labels (twelve of them), I sewed on using Mom's sewing machine. I only used it on clothes that had miter fold or book fold labels where I could sew my labels on the brand labels without showing through the skirt, blouse or slacks.

I used the sewing machine on Wednesday and Thursday evenings without any problems. Friday night however, Dad walked in on me and I freaked out.

I should have expected it since the sewing machine is Mom's and his bedroom. But recently he had been working late at his office at MIT, so I didn't expect him back at seven o'clock. Even if it was a Friday.

I was sitting at Mom's sewing desk and concentrating on the work, so I didn't hear him. I don't know how long he had been there, but he cleared his throat to let me know he was. He never came near me and hadn't closed the door. (If he had, I don't know what I would have done).

Anyway, I quickly lifted the pressure foot, cut the thread, grabbed the slacks I was working on and scooted out of there. I dodged around him staying out of his reach and ran for my bedroom.

Since most labels had to be sewn on by hand, though, I worked mostly in Karen's or my own bedroom.

When I was in Karen's, I sat on her bed, back against the headboard and legs stretched out and we chatted as I sewed. It was nice to just have some girl-talk time as well as time to discuss what had happened over that last week. Everything had moved so fast!

It was late Saturday night, when I finally sewed on the last label. I had used a good part of the labels Mrs. McCaffrey had made for me.

Scattered around me were the last of the clothes Karen and I had bought that afternoon, now all labeled and ready to be hauled to Willard. I glanced over at my alarm clock and saw it was one thirty in the morning.

I considered just raking the clothes off the bed and on to the floor, but decided not to. They would be really wrinkled in the morning and that would mean ironing them either tomorrow… Today really, or next week at school, before I could wear them.

So, I got up and hung up what needed to be hung up and folded what needed to be folded. That done, I collapsed on the bed and immediately went to sleep without even bothering to get under the covers.

Written the week of the 27th of March to the 1st of April, 1963.

April 1st, 1963

Dr. Jameson,

Uncle Roy called Sunday and said that Granny Roberts had alarmingly been going downhill since Grandpa died. He and Aunt May pretty much forced her to go see the doctor and he (the doctor) was very concerned and had her hospitalized. They're going to do a bunch of tests and x-rays on her this week.

I did get a got long conversation with Marty (much to Aunt May's displeasure). We talked almost ten minutes, though I'm pretty sure Aunt May listened in, so we had to be careful what we said.

With everything going on, is it silly to write about a week of clothes shopping? And about Karen sneakily getting a ball gown make for me? Is that just crazy?

Oh! I apologize about the Scots conversations, but at least I've been translating them into English!

Writing did distract me and I 'forgot' about everything for a while, which I guess is good.

Oh! I promise to make you copy of this account and leave it with the secretary tomorrow morning before classes begin, so you can read through it before my session. IF you have time, of course!

Sorry I haven't been doing that. I should have thought of that myself.

Sincerely yours,
Jenny

P.S. I meant having the copies made and leaving them for you with the secretary.

Journal: Sunday, September 3rd, 1961

MOVING IN DAY!

That morning, I slept in 'til almost eleven o'clock. I was surprised that neither Mom (or worse, Karen) had roused me out of bed yet.

All of my clothes, linens and school supplies were either hanging in my closet or folded in boxes or still in their original department store bags as the clerks had arranged them. Though for some things, stuffed would have been a more accurate word for their state than folded or arranged.

Anyway, I woke up to someone persistently banging on my door. When I heard Karen hollering at me to get up, I was justifiably leery, seeing as how she had recently been tossing me into cold showers while still dressed in my night gowns.

After waking up a little, I yelled back at her, asking what she wanted.

She replied that I needed to get up and come eat. That Mom had fixed me a special breakfast brunch and it was on the table.

I asked her if this was a trick to get me up so she could throw me in the shower again.

She laughed and responded that no, it wasn't a prank. That I needed to come on down and eat. Otherwise, the food was going to get cold.

I still wasn't sure, so I got up, went over to the door and cracked it open. Karen was standing there smiling and I thought that maybe this was 'on the up and up.'

However, I looked at her askance with squinty eyes and just to make sure, asked, "Promise?"

She laughed again and told me, "Yes, I promise," and then "Come on down, Sleepy Head."

The 'Sleepy Head' remark put me at ease, so I followed her down the hallway and stairs, and on to the kitchen.

When she told me Mom had fixed me a special meal, she wasn't joshing. There was a plate stacked with warm waffles, a quart jar of blackberries (probably canned by Grandmother), a tiny pitcher of maple syrup, butter on its dish, whipping cream (well, a can of Reddi Whip), a plate of crispy bacon and sizzling sausages, a big plate of scrambled eggs and a pitcher of orange juice.

Mom was taking some muffin outs of the oven. She smiled at me and said, "Blueberry muffins to snack on during the day when you get hungry."

I just stood there, speechless. I felt like crying and wondered what all my crying recently was about.

Mom saw I was getting teary-eyed and walked over to me and wrapped me in a wonderful hug. "I'm going to miss you too, Honey," she whispered to me.

I wasn't sure that was why I was so emotional. Maybe partly. I just couldn't think straight at that moment and in that situation.

Mom stepped back from me, put her hands on my shoulders, turned me towards the table and told me, "Have a seat, girl, and eat up!" Which I did.

As I dug into my food, quite unbidden, came the thought that I was glad Dad wasn't there. That would've ruined everything! My last breakfast before heading off to boarding school.

Then I realized that Mike wasn't there and for some weird reason, I wanted her to be. So, I asked Karen where she was and she replied, "I poked the bear in her den with the to-be-expected results!"

When Karen saw my disappointment, she smiled ruefully and said, "I'm sure she'll be down soon. I mean, smell this feast. How could she resist?"

The mood had turned a little somber, but it soon lightened up as Mom and Karen and I talked about family milestones: Us kids' first days in the first grade and funny happenings over the years.

Mom, with a wistful look, said, "All my little girls are growing up. Jenny leaving home to head off to school. Karen heading to college next year and Mike three years after that. Soon, it'll be just me and your Dad."

It felt like it was getting a little maudlin and I didn't even want to think about Dad at all. Especially about Mom being left alone with him. So, I jumped in to try to cheer Mom up a little.

"Mom, I'm not leaving home. I'll probably be back every weekend, whether you want me to or not! And I want you come up and have lunch or dinner with me at least once a week. You too, Karen."

Just at that moment, Mike came sleepily stumbling into the kitchen. "Wow, what a feast," she cheerfully commented, not at all her normal, grouchy self. "That bacon smells great!"

I looked at her in amazement and thought, 'Who are you and what have you done with my sister?'

Mike saw my expression and immediately snarked, "What?"

"Oh, nothing," I replied. "I'm just glad we're all eating breakfast together this morning." Except, thankfully not Dad, I added as a mental note to myself.

Mike may have been thinking the same thing, because she grinned with a smirk. Then without further comment or question, she piled up her plate and dug in.

Our conversation then wandered off into Karen's plans for the future. She wasn't sure which college she was going to apply to, torn between heading (far) away from home, like to a CUNY school in New York or staying closer to home in a UMass one.

Finally, near noon, Mom said, "I hate to break this up. We don't get to talk like this very often. I mean all of us. But… Jenny, you have a lot of packing to do and we need to head for Marblehead by four o'clock to have time to set up your room this evening."

I groaned, but got up and headed upstairs to go to work.

Then Mom turned to Karen and asked her, "Karen, can you help her and keep her on track?"

Karen chuckled and answered, "Sure, Mom."

As Karen and I were headed up the stairs, I heard Mom asking Mike, "Mike, can you help me with the dishes? It won't take long, but I need to get them done so I can help Jenny pack too."

"Not a problem," I heard Mike answer and then I heard the clinks of dishes being gathered up to wash them. (Gasp! By Mike?).

Again, I thought, 'What's up with my sister?'

With Karen's help (and later Mom's), I picked out the clothes that I would take with me for my first week at Willard. I knew that I didn't need to take everything. Just enough for a week or two. But I wasn't sure what I would need and what I wouldn't.

So, of course, I overpacked.

I wanted to bring the gown that Mrs. McCaffrey made for me to show Emalie and Sarah, but both Karen and Mom vetoed that. In the end, I packed all my school uniforms; a shirt dress; a pair of slacks; the two pairs of Mary Janes, a pair of sandals, my black pair of ballet flats and my tennis shoes; most of my lingerie; and some nylons and my blasted garter belt. I snuck in two pair of ruffled ankle socks to see if I could get away with not wearing nylons.

I considered bringing some bobby socks, but then thought better of it. I did sneak in a pair of shorts. (They weren't specifically forbidden in the student handbook, but I doubted I would be permitted to wear them). Under my lingerie, I also hid a Harvard logo tee shirt, which was specifically forbidden (a tee shirt, that is).

Then there were all my bed linens, my pillow and duvet, my little rug and my curtains. (I hoped there were good curtain rods. I hadn't thought to check when we looked at my room).

I was sure to not to forget my toiletries, my makeup, my bath robe, towels and wash cloths. (I wondered where we would be allowed to hang wet things to dry, though).

Last, but not least, was my Tiffany lamp!

All this fit in two big suitcases, a makeup case and four huge department store bags. The little prayer rug was just rolled up and the Tiffany was wrapped up in the old army blanket which Mom would take back home with her when she returned from Willard.

Needless to say, the station wagon was crammed to the gills. I wondered what parents with more than one daughter at Willard did.

We headed out for my new digs at four thirty (not TOO much behind schedule). Most of the new girls had arrived and hour or more before we did. (I found this out later, though).

Anyway, a little before six, Mom signed me in with Mrs. Finley. I signed for and received my key to the quad and my dorm room, with the warning that the loss of either one would cost me three dollars to have a door rekeyed. (Like it cost that much to put in a new lockset!).

Mom, Karen and I started ferrying up my stuff to my room. between the three of us it only took us two trips. Well, three for me. The third being to carry up the Tiffany Lamp. I didn't trust Mom or Karen with it. (Yeah, silly, I know).

Surprisingly, the rooms were squeaky-clean. The school had obviously hired people to clean the rooms. Windows, floors, walls, furniture and all.

While Mom busied herself with making my bed; Karen hung my shirts, pants and blazers on hangers; clipped my skirts on their hangers and hung everything in my armoire. She also arranged my shoes on its floor. I arranged my lingerie, socks and nylons in my chest-of-drawers.

I hadn't gotten ballet stuff from Mrs. Reynolds yet and worried about what I would wear to the class. I wondered if perhaps I should wear my shorts and my Harvard tee shirt, but ruled that out. No use in getting in trouble the first week of school!

Then, as I arranged my school supplies in my desk drawer and put my makeup case on my shelves, I realized that I hadn't brought any of my books (like novels!). Well, next weekend I'd bring some, I thought to myself. That or get Mom or Karen to bring some with them, if they came up for lunch or dinner during the week.

After we finished moving me in, Mom had to sign me back out to take me to dinner with her and Karen. When I mumbled that I thought that was pretty silly, Mrs. Finley heard me and informed me that she had had girls sneak out to go explore downtown Marblehead in the chaos of everyone moving in.

From that moment on until the end of the school year, she told me she expected to know where I, like all her girls, was at all times. Signing out and in was serious business, she let me know. [Me and my big mouth! I was going to have to be careful what I said around Mrs. Finley if I wanted to stay under her radar! Which I most certainly did!]

Mom took us to 'The Barnacle' again and we all had the same meal we had on the Wednesday of the entrance exam. Karen asked for Irish Coffee (again) and Mom told her absolutely not (again).

We got back to the dorm from our dinner at a little before nine o'clock and found Emalie still in the process of moving in. Mrs. Finley was standing outside our quad door in the hallway, looking on disapprovingly. (She was actually tapping the toe of her right foot on the floor as she stood there.).

Emalie had brought way too much stuff. She had no less than five medium-sized cardboard boxes stacked against the wall in her room. Later she told me that she had started to put them in the empty dorm room, but Mrs. Finley wouldn't let her.

Her reason? That there might be a late enrollment! Right! (That's not what Dr. Jameson had said! However, I kept my mouth shut. For once!).

Sarah took Emalie aside to whisper to her that she could move the boxes to the spare room after Mrs. Finley left. Which is what she did.

Getting ready for bed that evening was a madhouse. Everybody was hot and sweaty from the humidity and from hauling their stuff up to their rooms. (All the first and second years were on the second story).

At least Mrs. Finley didn't try to impose a 'lights out,' which we were told she sometimes did (despite 'lights out' not being mentioned in the student handbook! We weren't six-year-olds!).

After Sarah, Emalie and I got our showers (at almost eleven o'clock), we sat in the quad common room, drinking Cokes (sneakily bought downstairs) and talking until two o'clock in the morning.

I have to admit, I felt really grown up. For the first time in my life, I was on my own. (Well, sort of, anyway).

As we talked on and it cooled down, my feet started getting cold and I realized I had forgotten my 'bunny-eared' bedroom slippers! Oh well, next weekend. (Sigh…).

Written the week of the 3rd to the 8th of April, 1963.

April 8th, 1963

Dr. Jameson,

I know that this covers the time that you first suggested I write about (and more!), but I'd like to keep writing some more if that's okay with you.

Uncle Roy called Sunday afternoon with really bad news about Granny Roberts. She has advanced ovarian cancer. She should have seen to it months ago, but she said she was too occupied with Grandpa Roberts and she never had time "to go see some quack," in her words.

They're going to do an 'exploratory operation' on Tuesday. I want to meet with you, but I don't know how I will be feeling.

Sincerely,
Jenny

Journal: Monday, September 4th to Thursday, November 16th, 1961

My First Semester at Willard Academy to the Winter Ball

With my Mark Cross messenger bag crammed full of my notebooks, paper, pens, pencils and (a little) makeup; dressed in my new lingerie, my silk/cotton blend (boy's) blouse, wool skirt (kilt), wool blazer and black Mary Janes, I was ready to take on the world on my first day of school.

Along with all the other sixth graders, I was dressed in my new uniform according to the rules laid out in the student handbook. Along with my fellow first years, I didn't know any better. The returning students, however, all pretty much didn't bother to follow the dress code rules.

A lot of skirts were obviously too short. Along with my fellow sixth graders, I soon learned how you could roll your waist-band to raise your hemline, if that was 'what floated your boat.'

Personally, I don't see the point since there were no boys around to appreciate it. Gee whiz! It a girl's school! The only time I tried it was during the second week of school when I went to 'downtown' Marblehead (That's a joke!) with some other girls. I just did it to fit in. (Yeah, silly, I know).

I realized that with Marty not there, why should I bother? Really, I wasn't interested in flashing anyone! So, I didn't ever again do any 'rolling' (as Willard girls called it).

As the semester drew to an end, there was a bit of drama over the dress Mrs. McCaffrey made for me. As the time for the Winter Ball approached, all the 'Willardian' girls (except for me) got excited about what they were going to wear and more important, who their escorts were going to be.

I loved my gown and really appreciated of all the effort Karen, Mrs. McCaffrey and Mrs. Reynolds had gone to, making it for me. However…

The other girls' excitement only made me depressed. Most of them (truthfully, mostly only the high school girls) were being escorted by their boyfriends.

My boyfriend was more than a thousand miles away. I just

didn't feel like going to all the trouble of getting all dressed up, having my face made up and getting my hair done for anyone but Marty.

I thought about this hard and long. Was Marty my boyfriend? I mean, we had been best friends forever. Well, for five years, which IS forever for an eleven-year-old. I always signed my letters to him 'With all my love.' Well, with 'Avec tout mon amour,' which means the same thing in French.

But that was what he told me to write when I asked him how I should sign my letters in French.

I had never thought about it. What did HE mean by that?

He always signed his letters to me with 'Je t'aime.' Which means, of course, 'I love you.'

As I kept thinking about it, I asked myself, 'What IS a friend?' Then with unusual clarity, I realized I had a lot of girls (and a few boys) I was friendly with, but only one 'true friend.'

Moreover, I only saw that 'friend' for one week each year. Had I used our special relationship as a 'modus operandi' to keep people at an arm's length? To avoid other meaningful relationships?

More disturbingly, I asked myself, 'Does that make me a bad person?' Was I a bad person? All this pondering distracted me from my depression, but answers to these questions stumped me.

Then like 'un coup de foudre' ('a bolt of lightning,' literally; but also, figuratively, 'to fall in love at first sight'), I knew that not only was Marty my boyfriend, but also, I might be in love with him! (Gasp!).

But he was my cousin! That ought to have been even more reason to be depressed, but I didn't feel depressed about it. I felt good. Or, at least, better!

About a week before the ball, Emalie asked me who was going to be my escort and when I said I didn't plan on going, you would have thought I said I was going to off myself!

She jumped all over me, lecturing me on all the reasons that I was, I quote, "Being stupid!"

She told me:

1. I was pretty;
2. Any number of boys had to be standing in line to ask to be my escort. (I didn't ask who, but it would have been interesting to know!);
3. I had an absolutely gorgeous gown;
4. My hair, unlike her 'mousy brown,' was a gorgeous golden copper color (both were untrue in my opinion and anyway, what color is 'golden copper'?);
5. Karen would really be upset with me (which was, unfortunately, all too true);
6. I would be absolutely ungrateful to not go, after all the trouble she (Karen) had gone to;
7. The Ball was Willard's most important social event of the year!' (except for the Spring Ball, which was, of course, equal to other high schools' senior proms);
8. That, unlike her, I didn't have nor had I ever had a zit! (which, unfortunately for her, was true. At that time, she this big red zit on her chin. Also, she was right about me not having zits. I didn't remember ever having had a zit, but then, I really hadn't yet hit puberty either);
9. Lastly and the most troubling, Marty would want me to go and have some fun. (This was true, but I would feel guilty. I know if Marty went to some dance with a girl, I would definitely be upset. Read: 'jealous').

When she ran out of steam, Sarah, who had heard the row and wandered in, eagerly waited to join in on it. She was about to let me know what she thought, but I cut her off…

"Look. The only BOY I want to take me to the Ball is now a thousand miles away!"

"Jenny, you don't have to have an escort. There'll be lots of boys there to dance with," Sarah reasoned. "A lot, if not most, of the first and second years won't have dates."

"Will you," I asked.

"Well, yes…" she answered.

"You will!" Emalie exclaimed. "Who?"

"Oh. You don't know him," Sarah told her with a twinkle

in her eye, full well knowing that Emalie would never let it go with just that bit of information.

"Is he a 'local'?" she pressed Sarah.

"No. He's from Allston," Sarah replied.

"Then how's he going to get here?" Emalie asked with surprise.

"Oh. By car," Sarah answered matter-of-factly.

"You're dating a sixteen-year-old guy!" Emalie gasped, but then looked at Sarah sharply.

Sarah coyly held her peace.

"Does your Mom know this boy is taking you to the dance?" Emalie interrogated Sarah.

"Walking me over to the gym is no big deal," Sarah said to needle Emalie. "But yes, Mom knows Aaron is taking me to the ball," she went on.

Emalie scrutinized Sarah closely and then asked, "Are you going anywhere… after the ball?"

"As a matter of fact…" Sarah began, but Emalie cut her off disgustedly, "You're lying!"

That was all Sarah could take and she burst out laughing. When she finally got herself under control, she explained, "Aaron is twelve and he is coming BY CAR, but his cousin, who's dating a senior here, is driving. Furthermore, the four of us are leaving the Ball at ten to go get some desert. At 'The Barnacle,' before you ask, Emalie."

"Furthermore," she went on with a smirk, "Mom wrote a letter to Mrs. Hovhaness giving me permission to come home from the Ball without having to sign out and in and out again like Mrs. Finley wanted."

"So there! Everything I told you was the exact truth. You just jumped to conclusions!" Sarah finished off with a flourish.

Emalie was trying to look angry, but when I burst out laughing, so did she. Raising her hands in the air, she just said, "Oh you!"

Sarah was on a roll, though, and asked Emalie, "Who's going to be your escort?"

With a grin, Emalie answered, "Well, if you must know…" inserting a long pause for dramatic effect, before going on, "Why Jenny, of course!"

"What!" I squeaked.

"Listen Jenny, like Sarah said, there'll be lots of boys there and not all of them with their girlfriends. Some may even be coming with their cousins!"

I didn't respond (verbally) to her dig. I just rolled my eyes.

"Really, Jenny, there'll be lots of boys who would be more than happy to dance with you," Sarah backed Emalie up.

"You guys don't understand. I don't want to dance with anyone…" I hesitated before finishing, "but Marty."

There was a pregnant pause at my avowal. Sarah and Emalie looked at each other and Sarah nodded knowingly to Emalie before they both looked back at me.

Then, at the same time, both said, "So…" but halted before going on.

It was Sarah that broke the silence. She looked over at Emalie and said, "I told you so!"

Emalie turned back towards her and admitted, "Yeah, you did."

After another long pause, Sarah commented, "It happens a lot more in Europe. One summer, Mom and Dad and I went to the wedding of a close friend of Mom's daughter. Did I say that right?" Sarah asked.

"I don't think so," Emalie replied, "because I don't understand what you meant, unless it was YOUR friend?"

"Let me begin again. Mom's friend's daughter was getting married and it was to her cousin. Is that clear or at least clearer?" Sarah asked us.

"I think so," Emalie replied, but then contradicted herself, "No. Not really."

"Let me re-begin all over then. The wedding was in Austria. In Salzburg. I was only eight-years-old, but I remember it was beautiful," Sarah looked dreamy-eyed, but then straightened up her expression and went on with her story.

"Anyway, someone told me the bride was marrying her cousin. So… I asked who was 'her'?" Sarah took a breath and then continued, "The woman who told me was some distant cousin of Mom's and she was Austrian. She had this heavy German accent, so I thought maybe it was some language mix-up.

"As it was hard to understand the woman, I asked Mom what the woman had just said. Mom explained that the bride was marrying her own cousin. The bride's own cousin. There. Got that?" Sarah asked looking pointedly at Emalie.

When Emalie nodded 'yes,' Sarah went on, "Anyway, I asked Mom wasn't that weird. Marrying your cousin. And she said that no, it was pretty common in Europe. I wasn't sure about that, so I asked some of the kids my age at the wedding about it.

"They all wanted to practice their English with me all the time, which was fine with me since I didn't speak German. Only a little Yiddish," Sarah wandered off into extraneous details. Again!

I was getting annoyed and wanted Sarah to go ahead and finish her story and make her point and leave me alone!

"So, what did the kids say?" I asked pointedly.

"They didn't understand what I was asking at first," Sarah replied.

"I wonder why?" I remarked sarcastically.

"I don't know," she replied (like she hadn't recognized my sarcasm).

"That was a rhetorical question," I told her. Sarah's pretty smart, but storytelling didn't seem to be her 'forte' or so I thought at that time.

Anyway, Sarah plowed on ahead, "They didn't think it was in any way a big deal and asked me why I was so interested. Well, I told them I thought cousins getting married was weird and that they couldn't get married in America.

"They didn't know the word 'weird,' so we had to get Mom to translate for us. In German it's 'seltsam.' Strange that I remember that! Seltsam!" Sarah remarked wistfully.

"And so?" I remarked pointedly.

"When the kids finally understood what I was saying and that cousins couldn't get married in America, they thought it was hilarious. 'Who ever heard of such a thing!' they asked and died laughing."

"I was so embarrassed! No eight-year-old girl wants to be laughed at by kids her own age! Though strictly, they weren't really laughing at me."

"Later I talked to Mom about it and she tried to explain to me the idea of customs. That different people had different customs. I could see that. But that particular customs could be good or bad. Or both good and bad. Or neither good or bad, like neutral. All that was completely beyond what I could understand at eight-years-old."

"Mom did tell me that while many states in America wouldn't permit cousins to get married, some did. Like Massachusetts," Sarah told me.

Like 'un coup de foudre' when it just means 'suddenly,' I got the suspicion that Sarah's rambling, naïve recounting of her experience at the wedding (if it really happened at all) was in reality 'une pièce de théâtre comique' (a dramatic comedy) staged for my benefit.

Actually, if that dialogue was extemporaneous, she should try out for leads in the school dramas! She had told the story so naturally and believably.

I decided to just act like she had taken me in, but also to throw her a curve with a 'redirect.' That's a 'behavior management strategy' (distracting a young child from misbehaving by enticing her into an alternative, acceptable activity). Like not talking about Marty and me being cousins!

Psychology, useful stuff sometimes!

I went on, "Like I said before, getting boys to dance with me is something I could care less about."

"But…" Emalie began, only to be cut off by Sarah. "There will be a lot of girls going stag, not just mouses and wallflowers."

"Watch it!" Emalie grumbled. "I'm not a mouse!"

"I didn't mean to suggest you were," Sarah replied sweetly (too sweetly!).

"Anyway," she went on, "some of the girls who are the best dancers go stag on purpose. Not because they can't get a date, but because it would be a drag for them to be paired the whole evening with some clod hopper who can't follow their moves."

"Sarah's right about that. The best dancers dance solo a lot. To the fast music, anyway. It would be sort of creepy for then to dance to slow songs that way, though."

"And why's that?" Sarah challenged her.

"It's too much 'Oh look at me! I'm sexy!' You know, putting on a show," Emalie said and then stood up swiveling her hips and waving her hers over her head to demonstrate her idea (not too successfully).

Sitting back down, Emalie then went on, "That's okay on stage. Like for modern dance." She nodded to me, but then continued, "But in the middle of a bunch of couples. Ew!"

"Maybe you're right about that," Sarah conceded.

"Sometimes I like to dance with a group, without an obvious partner. With just girls. That happened a lot when the boys at the dance were mostly duds. That was always the case at the dances at Thomas Gardner," Emalie grimaced at the memory.

Surprised, Sarah asked, "Why ever would you go to a dance at Thomas Gardner?"

"That's where I went to school," Emalie frowned with her admission.

"Wow! That's awful!" Sarah exclaimed and then realized her faux-pas. "Sorry, I didn't mean..." she started to apologize, but Emalie cut her off, "No. You're right. It was awful!"

"If you don't mind me asking, why did you go there?"

"Mom and Dad wanted me to go to a 'public school in our community,' to use their words."

"But... didn't they know. You know. About the school's reputation?"

"Not at first, but I gave them an earful at every chance I got! It was only when the school finally was ordered to tell the parents about a kid being savagely beaten up by some bullies and hospitalized, that they paid attention."

"I heard about that. Didn't the kid suffer brain damage?"

"Yeah, he did. After that, at least one of them went to every PTA meeting. When they heard the complaints of other parents, they started taking my 'whining,' as they called it, seriously."

"And let you come to Willard?"

"Yeah. They finally caved. But they still think that my experience of 'dealing with kids from other socio-economic classes,' as they put it, would 'broaden my horizons and build character.' What a joke!"

"Wow! They sound like dyed in the wool, bleeding heart

liberals!”

'Sarah needed to get a better filter!' I thought. 'Talk about hoof-in-mouth disease!'

Sarah realized her faux-pas again and quickly added, “Not that being a progressive and caring about inequality is a bad thing!”

“We get regular doses of that at every dinner. You can ask Jenny about that!”

“I thought that your Mom and Dad were pretty right-on in their politics!” I defended them.

Treading more carefully, Sarah asked, “What do they do for a living? Are they in politics?”

“No. They’re criminal defense lawyers,” Emalie grimaced again. For what, I couldn’t see.

Sarah just remarked with a knowing and drawn out, “Ooohhh.”

I saw the politics might be a touchy topic with Emalie and Sarah. Something to avoid.

Emalie’s face grew darker and she said, “They plan on leaving my sister, Heike, at Thomas Gardner until she can start here in a year and a half.”

“I’m sure she’ll be okay,” I told Emalie, but wasn’t at all sure that was the case.

“She probably will. She’s not as much of a trouble-marker as I am. She’s never even been called to the principal’s office. Not even once!”

'And you have?' I thought and then, 'I wonder how often and why?'

I quickly decided, 'I don’t want to know and I’m not going to ask. If she wants me to know she can tell me.'

Without looking over at me, Sarah expressed a sympathetic, “I’m sure she’ll be fine.”

I thought this chat had gone on along this line far enough, so to lighten things up, I told them, “Well, about the dance… You two’ve talked me into it. I’ll go, but I refuse to dance with any boys.”

Second homerun for 'redirects!'

Emalie did cheer up at my decision and told me, “That’s great, Jenny! It’ll be a blast. You’ll see! We can help each other get ready. With our hair and make-up. We won't have any classes after fourth period on Friday. That'll give us plenty of time, won't it, Sarah?"

Sarah hesitated before answering and when she did it was in a somewhat apologetic voice, "Ahh. I'm getting my hair done at the beauty parlor in town." However, without dropping a beat, she continued more sunnily, "But I'd really like to help you with your hairdos. And we can all help each other with our makeup too!"

Not wanting to upset Emalie or put Sarah on the spot, I jumped in, "That sounds great! Oh, and what are you going to wear? You've seen my gown. Are yours here?"

They both leaped up and talking over each other, told me, "Mine's in my armoire," (Emalie) and "Mine's hanging in my room." (Sarah).

We all laughed at that and they went to get their dresses.

Emalie's was a stylish L.B.D. (little black dress) in satin with a black lace overlay. The neckline was a 'bateau' (boat) cut and the hemline was above the knee (well above the knee!).

It was definitely a cocktail dress and being sleeveless, not really practical for the Winter Ball. It being, of course, in WINTER!

Unless the gym was really heated well (which it had never yet been), she was going to freeze. It was sexy, though, but in my eyes a little 'mature' for Emalie's eleven years.

Sarah came out carrying a burgundy colored, floor length gown with a brocade skirt and a bodice completely covered with sequins. Like Emalie's dress, it was sleeveless.

She handed me the gown saying, "Here, hold this for me. I'll be right back."

She went back in her room and closed her door. A minute later, she opened her door and stepped in the doorway. In very high heels with her left hip tilted up and her right leg out to the side in a suggestive pose, she placed her hands on her hips.

Over her shoulders was an elbow length fur cape of white, blond, rust and gray fur running in lengthwise pelts. Little flecks of heart-shaped, black fur were scatted over the lighter shades.

Emalie's and my jaws must have dropped at the sight.

Emalie was the first to be able to breathe enough to be able to speak. "Is that yours? What kind of fur is that? Can I touch it? Can I try it on? I mean, put it on my shoulders?" She spewed out her questions machine-gun rapid without giving Sarah the chance to respond.

Sarah laughed and answered, "No, it's my Mom's. It's American Lynx. And yes, and yes. I mean you have to touch it if you try it on!"

Emalie tossed her dress onto one of the settees and ran, not walked, over to Sarah. She reached out and ran her fingers down the collar. "It's so soft. Not like my fluffy teddy bear at all!"

When she realized what she had just said, she dropped her hand and turned bright red. "Sorry! That was dumb!" In more of a comment than an apology.

Sarah smiled at her, told her to turn around and then placed the cape on her shoulders.

Emalie looked surprised and gasped, "It's so light. I'm mean it's so thick. I was expecting it to be heavy!"

"I know. I was surprised, too, when I first put it on," Sarah agreed.

"Did your Mom give it to you?"

"I wish! But no. Dad gave it to her for her birthday. It's like, brand new. She's just letting me borrow it for the Ball."

Emalie ran both her hands down the mostly white collar from her collarbone to her hips, "Wow! I'm so jealous! Jenny gets a fur coat of her own, even if it is beaver. Then you get to borrow this from your Mom for the Ball!"

"What do you mean? 'Even if it is beaver!' It's got a red fox collar and cuffs!" I pursed my lips, but couldn't keep from grinning.

"You know what I mean!" Emalie looked askance at me. Then this look of wistful longing came over her face as she looked down and lifted the collar to her nose and smelled it with her eyes closed.

Dropping the collar back into place, she looked over to Sarah and said, "There's almost no smell. Only a slight perfume-like scent."

"That's probably Mom's perfume. I don't think there's any

smell on new furs. It's only if you don't take care of them that they get that musty smell." Sarah then turned to me and asked, "Do you want to try it on?"

"I would like to see how much it weighs in comparison to mine," I told her and laid her gown across the back of the settee beside me.

"Emalie?" Sarah asked indicating that she wanted to take the fur back.

"Oh. Sure," Emalie responded as Sarah took the cape off her shoulders.

Sarah stepped over to me, asked me to turn around and placed the cape on my shoulders like she had for Emalie. It was amazingly light. I think a cape the same size made out of beaver would weight more, but due to the differences in sizes of my coat and her cape, it was hard to judge.

The lynx fur, though, was a lot softer than my beaver. That was for sure. But that meant it was probably more fragile, too. I was happier with my coat. It was more practical. The cape was really only for 'posh dos' as the Brits call their society events.

I took a step back so Sarah could take the cape back and thanked her for letting me try it on.

As she headed back to her room, I picked up her gown and followed her.

She laid the cape on her bed, slipped off her heels and put them in her armoire. Then she picked up a cloth garment bag lying there on her bed, took her gown from me and slipped the garment bag over it. Then after zipping the bag up, she carefully hung her gown up.

Then she took this shorter cloth bag, zipped it open and pulled it off of this huge padded coat hanger. Arranging the cape on the hanger, she then slipped the bag over it, zipped the bag up, and hung the cape up right next to her gown.

"You really take care of your clothes, don't you," I asked.

"I haven't thought about it, but yeah, I guess I do," she replied.

"Do you always put the fur and your gown in garment bags? I mean I'm asking if I should get a bag for my coat and my gown. To be truthful. I've never owned anything like either of them before."

"For the gown, that depends on how long you think you can wear it," Sarah answered. "The bag does keep it from getting dusty. But for furs, they always need to be hung in bags since it's so expensive to clean them.

"Mom lectured and lectured me before she let me borrow it. If something happened to it, she would kill me. She told me to let it air out before putting it in its bag and hanging it in my closet. Ev-er-ry time!"

"And if, heaven forbid, I get any rain or sweat on it. Or even 'expose it to heavy fog,' I'm to wipe it off with this soft terrycloth hand towel she gave me and let it air until it's 'absolutely dry' before bagging it and hanging it in my closet!"

"Huhn. Do you mean if I get mine wet, I can't just hang mine up in my armoire to dry? That's what I've been doing."

"That's a definite no-no! Mom told me that here at school, I should hang it on the hook on the wall, but at home she has a special clothes rack so it can hang and dry on all sides. She said she would let me 'get away' with hanging it on a hook here because it wouldn't be here that long!"

"And also, the bag needs the be a breathable fabric. Like cotton and never a waterproof one," Sarah added.

"Maybe I don't really want a fur coat. It sounds like just too much trouble!" Emalie remarked. Sarah and I turned towards her. We had been unaware she was listening to us. She was standing in the doorway, leaning against the door jamb.

"But they're so beautiful. They're worth the trouble," Sarah commented.

Emalie just shrugged and said, "Different folks, different strokes!"

I smiled at her and said, "I'll have to tell Marty that saying. I doubt he knows it!"

Sarah and Emalie looked at each other and rolled their eyes.

"What?" I asked.

"Oh, nothing," Sarah replied.

I could tell that Emalie wanted to say something else, but she didn't.

In her own 'redirect,' Sarah asked me, "So... You're definitely coming to the dance?" Then in a fake 'posh' British accent, while bending her wrist with her hand held forward, she said, "I mean the Ball!"

I grimaced and replied, "Yeah, I guess so."

"Well, Good... But now... I've got a math test to study for." Signaling that the fun and games were over for the evening and she wanted us to scoot so she could study.

I screwed up my face and said, "Well, I think I'm going on to bed. The ballet classes leave me absolutely exhausted."

"Poor you!" Emalie stuck out her bottom lip and repeatedly batted her eyes in (simulated!) sympathy.

I reached for Sarah's pillow to throw at her. But Emalie ran for her room and Sarah grabbed the pillow away from me before I could throw it, anyhow.

I pulled a wry face at Sarah and slouched off to my room to grab my shower caddy. After the hassle of taking my shower and drying my hair, I was more than exhausted. I crashed on my bed and was asleep in moments.

Written the week of the 10th to the 15th of April, 1963.

Monday, April 15th, 1963

Dr. Jameson,

As you heard, my Granny Roberts died yesterday. Ironically on Easter, the Day of Resurrection. At least this time, Uncle Roy let Mom know immediately. He wasn't going to depend on Aunt May to do it (or not do it) like when Grandpa died.

I don't remember if I told you that Granny had ovarian cancer and not uterine like the doctor first thought. When they did the exploratory surgery, they found that it had spread all over her abdomen including around her uterus. It was inoperable and they just sewed her back up, expressing wonder at how she had stood the pain.

Mom's flying this afternoon to Nashville. She gave Karen, Mike and me the choice of going, without thinking it through. Mike right-out refused. Since she did, Karen couldn't go and leave Mike to her own devices.

I wanted to go, but Mom asked me to HONESTLY tell her WHY I wanted to go and like a dummy I answered truthfully. I wanted to see Marty.

Then she said that since I hadn't gone to Grandpa Roberts's funeral, I probably shouldn't go to Granny's funeral either. Merde! Excuse my French!

I hadn't finished up this week's missive, so I skipped classes today and completed it. I'm still out of sorts, but I don't feel sad. Honestly, I don't understand what I feel. It's more like I'm just completely exhausted.

Before Mom left, she dropped a bombshell. She said that since both Grandpa and Granny had died, we might not have the reunion this year! Marty and I have been there every year since we were seven!

That means that I won't see Marty until the end of August when he comes to live with us. (Yeah! Well, yeah, he's going to live with us, but Boo! Not until almost September!).

I'm leaving my missive and this letter with the secretary like last week. They'll be there when you come in tomorrow.

Sincerely yours,
Jenny

159

Journal: Friday, November 17th, 1961

The Winter Ball

On the day of the Ball, the Friday before Thanksgiving, it was like all the girls were high on amphetamines. I really pitied the teachers. Hardly anyone was really paying attention to them.

Several girls in my classes got caught passing notes, which our teachers made them read out loud to the whole class. They were all silly notes like 'Are you excited?' or 'Can I borrow that new lipstick from you. You know, the cherry red one?' or 'Who's going to be your escort?' Important stuff. (Not!).

It was good we only had classes through fourth period. Because yeah! No ballet! (My ballet class was fifth period, just after lunch).

I was afraid that Madame Roget was going to make us come to ballet even though all classes after lunch had officially been canceled. I wouldn't have put it past her. She is really strict. A slave-driver!

But she said that since we would be dancing all that evening, we wouldn't meet. However, she warned us to not let "the contemporary, popular dance styles" affect our 'form' which we had "worked on so strenuously all fall!" That our ballet classes should 'inform' our dance movements in all styles!

I could just see all the ballet students holding themselves "straight and tall" with their "spinal columns all the way to the top their head straight like a pillar of a Greek temple!" (Madame Roget's constant instruction / lecture / nagging!).

Like anyone would dance a slow song without putting her head on her boyfriend's shoulder!

After lunch Emalie wanted us to start working on our hair or rather start having our hair 'worked on.' The only thing I did in preparation was rinse mine out that morning and the previous morning, and in the afternoon, after ballet class. Experience had taught me that if I didn't shampoo my hair for the couple of days before I curled it with a curling iron, the curls looked nicer and lasted longer.

That day, the shower room was like Grand Central Station

at rush hour. There were official queues and heaven preserve the girl that tried to cut in before her allotted time!

A number of girls just gave up and washed their hair in the lavatories if they couldn't get an early enough shower time. (There was actually a time sheet to sign up on and reserve a time slot!).

I just saw it as a way to avoid spending any more time than I had to, (was being forced to), primping for the Ball. My late slot meant that Sarah had to leave for the beauty salon before I took my shower.

The whole set up bears explanation. Everyone has to sign for a time slot. Each person gets fifteen minutes and not a second more unless the person before them doesn't use all their time. (This is 'as rare as hens' teeth' as Aunt May would say).

I asked, but no one knew how the system got started. Everyone said it had been the routine 'forever.' That there had always been a time sheet to shower on the afternoons of the Winter and the Spring Balls. Furthermore, it was organized by the girls themselves with no involvement of the administration.

I guess it does avoid a lot of screaming, or worse, 'cat fights.' I had to give them that.

Anyway, my slot was three o'clock and I didn't do more than a cursory shower (with my hair in a shower cap), so I finished before ten minutes of my time had gone by. (Maybe 'hen's teeth' do exist!). I'm sure the girl following me appreciated the five extra minutes.

When I got back to our quad, Emalie was rolling her hair in these huge hair rollers using a small mirror on a stand to see what she was doing. When she saw me, she exclaimed, "Oh good! You're back! I could use some help. It's hard to see what I'm doing like this."

"Why don't you use the mirror in your room?" I asked.

She rolled her eyes at my lack of common sense and asked, "How could I do anything without a table right there to put all my hair stuff on?" The table in the common room was covered with her hair pins, brushes, elastic hair bands, barrettes, a big and a small curling iron and a plastic box with hair rollers standing on end in it.

When I just stood there without answering, she got peeved

and asked, "Well, are you going to help me?"

"I don't know how," I responded. "I've never used hair rollers."

"Never?" she asked, not finding that credible.

"Nope. Never," I assured her.

"But your hair. It's gorgeous. What do you do to fix it up?"

"I shampoo it or rinse it. Comb it out. Dry it. Brush it. That's all," I replied.

"What conditioner do you use."

"Johnson's Baby Shampoo."

"No. I mean conditioner. Like a crème rinse."

"I guess I don't use one. I just use Johnson's Baby Shampoo."

Emalie looked at me like I was crazy and then looked dubious and asked, "You're not kidding, are you?"

"No, I've always used just Johnson's…"

"Baby Shampoo," she cut me off.

"Well, Mom always used it when I was a little kid, but when I was seven, she told me I was going to have to start shampooing my own hair by myself.

"Well, I tried some of Karen's shampoo, but it got in my eyes and really stung. So, I went right back to Johnson's…"

"Baby Shampoo," she finished my sentence for me.

"Yeah."

"And you don't use any conditioner?" she asked again.

"Nope."

This wasn't exactly the whole truth. Once in a while, I now washed my hair with a mixture of shampoo and baking soda. It was a trick my grandmother taught me to clean any hairspray residue from my hair. No way was I telling this to Emalie, though. She already thought I was weird about my hair.

"How do you keep your hair from flying away when it's windy?" she asked.

"It just doesn't. Not any more than other girls' I guess."

"Do you use a lot of hairspray then?" she asked.

"No, not much. I don't like the way it makes my hair feel. Though now with ballet, I do have to use a little. You know to fix my chignon."

"Chignon?"

"You know, the dancer's bun? You've seen me in it after ballet."

"Yeah… But back to your hair. You don't use conditioner. You don't use hardly any hair spray. But your hair always looks good. Not dry and not oily either. It's just not fair!" Emalie grouched.

"Both Mike's and Karen's hair is oilier than mine and they have to use stronger shampoos or wash their hair twice. If I used their shampoos, I think it would mess my hair up. It would be a fly away mess," I opined.

Then I went on, "Karen ran out of shampoo once and borrowed mine. But it was too mild and didn't cut oil in her hair. She even shampooed her hair twice and was still not happy with it.

"She ended up having to use soap to wash her hair, but that dried her hair out too much. So, then she had to condition her hair twice.

"She wasn't a happy camper, but I wasn't either. She had used up all my shampoo! So, I made her replace my shampoo before that next morning."

"I have to do a lot of work on my hair to keep it nice. That's why I get up early on school days. To wash my hair and fix it up. As well as to get my makeup right," Emalie let me know.

"I always wait until the last minute. But it doesn't take me long to wash (or rinse, I didn't say), comb, dry and brush my hair. I don't use much makeup either. Just a little and some tinted lip balm. Sometimes not even that.

"However, I do my hair two times a day now. I have to with ballet. I get so sweaty and don't want to leave the hair spray in my hair all evening and night. So, I rinse my hair out after ballet.

"Oh shoot! I must have pulled the plug out on the rollers. The dots turned red!" Emalie complained.

"The dots turned red?" I asked, not understanding.

Emalie pointed to dots on her rollers, "See the red dots? When the rollers are hot, they turn black," she explained.

Emalie unrolled one of her rollers and as she was doing the second one, she asked me, "Can you plug the roller heater back in for me?"

"Sure," I said and hunted down the plugin and stuck it back in the wall socket.

When I turned back around, Emalie was brushing out the curls from the two rollers. I looked over the roller heating box and asked, "So, hot rollers?" (Duh! Talk about a stupid question with an answer I already knew!).

"Yeah. It's a new set. The rollers have wax cores, so they hold their heat longer. They give a better set. Faster too."

"Uh, Emalie. I've never used rollers. Ever. Not even the spongy ones like Karen uses," I told her and then went on (no way did I want to be corralled into doing her hair!).

"I mean she starts with wet hair and lets it dry with the rollers on. That would have to be uncomfortable, besides being a big hassle. So, I've never been interested."

"Really?" Emalie asked. "But you had curls when we first went to Marblehead together. And I think when you came over to dinner too. How did you get them?"

"I get Mom or Karen to use a curling iron when I do up my hair," I replied. "Those times it was Karen."

"Have you ever watched Karen from start to finish when she used rollers?"

"No. Why would I?"

"Well, according to Mom, little sisters are 'always' interested in watching their older sisters get dressed up. Recently, Heike has been a real pest and when I complained to Mom, she said it's only natural that little sisters want to 'observe' their Moms and older sisters. To just ignore her!"

"There's no way I would want to 'observe' Mike, even if she would let me. The less I'm around her, the better!"

"What about Karen?"

"There's just too much difference in our ages. We're not at all interested in the same things. Anyway, I wouldn't want to bug her."

"I wouldn't want to bug my Mom either, but I think for a different reason than you with Karen. Mom can be like a drill sergeant. I think it comes from being a woman in a man's profession. She says that she has to be tough and have a 'thick skin,' or she'll get walked over. So, I tend to avoid Mom.

Maybe not like you do Mike, but we aren't buddy-buddy at all."

"Mom and I aren't buddy-buddy, either, I guess. But we do have a good relationship. I know I can talk to her, well, about most anything."

'Except about Dad,' I thought to myself, but I went on, "When I was younger and, well, even now, when I want to talk, I get her to brush my hair. Not really to just brush it, but to talk too."

"The only reason I get Mom to comb my hair is to comb my hair! Recently, we just don't talk..." Emalie paused thoughtfully, but then went on, "Anyway, talking about hair. I don't get the impression that you want to work on my hair."

I grimaced and answered honestly, "Sorry, but not really. In any case, I would be afraid I'd mess it up."

"Well, I know that you put your hair in a bun every day for ballet, but you do need to learn how to do your hair up for fancy occasions, too."

"Look," she went on, "let me just give you some basics. You don't really want your hair 'soaking wet,' just damp, when you use hot rollers."

"Anyway, if you've just taken a shower, you just towel your hair dry until it's just damp. If you haven't just showered, should just spray mist your hair until it's damp before rolling it in the hot rollers."

Emalie continued, "I won't go into how to roll your hair for different styles. That would take hours!" I thought she was finishing up, but she bulldozed on instead.

"Anyway, as you take your hair down, you just spritz it with hair spray to help hold the volume and curls. Then gently brush it. If you brush it too hard or too much, you'll lose both the body and the curls."

"Thanks, Emalie. But I don't think I want to use rollers, hot or otherwise. I just don't like bouffant, beehives or flips and those seem to be what rollers are mostly used for. If I do anything with my hair besides brushing it, I use a curling iron."

Just at that moment, Sarah got back from the hair salon. Her hair was done in a modest updo and a flip forward on the bottom. Sort of like how Jackie Kennedy wore her hair. Sarah's hair style was much more modest than I was expecting.

Immediately, Sarah was drafted into working on Emalie's hair and although she kept toning down Emalie's ideas, Emalie pushed back and ended up with a much more elaborate coiffure than Sarah's. An elaborate half updo with dramatic waves, soft curls and face-framing ringlets. Hard to describe, but very princessy!

Thankfully, Sarah took so much time on Emalie's hairdo, there wasn't much time left to torture me. Getting right to it, she told me to go into her room and have a seat on her desk chair.

Following me, she stepped over to her chest-of-drawers, opened a drawer and started digging through it. She pulled out a couple of packages of sheer, nylon, panty-tights. I wondered what she was up to. What did nylons have to do with fixing my hair?

Both the nylons were shades of reddish brown. She took a look at each, glancing at me in turn and then put one of them back in the drawer. Stepping over to me, she held up the other pair (of a medium rust color) next to my temple to compare it to my hair, I supposed.

"Not an exact match, but close enough," she commented and then she tore open the package, took out the pair of the panty-tights and handed them to me. I had no idea why and just waited on her to explain herself.

Tossing the packaging on her desk, she opened one of her desk drawers pulled out a pair of scissors and asked me to hold up one leg by its foot and waistband on the same side and stretch them out!

"Que est-ce que tu fous?" I asked, so flabbergasted I didn't even realize I was swearing at her in French. Which, of course, she couldn't understand.

"Hunh?" she asked with raised eyebrows.

It took me a couple of seconds to realize what I had done and translated what I had said, "That means 'what in the hell are you thinking' dammit!"

"I'm cutting off a leg," she answered calmly, ignoring the rudeness of my outburst.

I held the panty-tights out of her reach and squealed, "But these are brand new!" I looked over at the package and saw that the tights were Christian Dior's! And what's more, they cost two dollars!

"Es tu dingue? Ça coute deux dollars!" I went off in French again. "Sorry!" I apologized. Regrettably, however, I went on, "But are you crazy? Those cost two dollars!" Translating without admitting it, I didn't want to apologize twice!

"I sort of understood what you were saying, but please, for now, just go along with me," she pled.

"It's hard to explain everything, but I need the tube part of a leg to make a hair ratt, shaped like a donut. And before you ask, I'm talking about a 'hair form' to make buns and not a rodent!"

I gave in and held the leg of the panty-tights so she could cut off the foot and then cut off the leg just below where it was attached to the panties. After that she rolled the tubular leg until it is scrunched up into a donut shape. Like you do when you roll hose to put them on. It did look like a donut. Sort of, I guess.

She told me she was going to plait an upside down, French braid from my neck up and then make a high bun like I did for ballet.

First, she teased my hair and sprayed it with hairspray. Then she had me bend forward so she could comb my hair forward. Then she plaited a tight French braid. Once she reached the upper part of the back of my head, she simply tied off the end of the braid with a hair elastic.

I told her that was more comfortable than the rubber bands I used for my ballet buns. Which brought on a lecture about how rubber bands were bad for hair, because they pull on it and that causes breakage. (Horrors!).

Then she combed my hair back from my face (adding more hairspray, sigh), gathered it with the ponytail at the end of the braid and added another elastic making a big, high ponytail like I do for my ballet buns.

That's where the ratt came in. Instead of just twisting my hair around the base of the ponytail to make a bun (with the addition of a bunch of bobby pins to hold it in place), she started at the end of the ponytail!

Tucking my hair into the 'ratt' (I'm not sure how, since I couldn't see it being done, as Sarah was holding my hair up above my head), she then rolled it (the ratt) down.

As I said before, the 'ratt' was 'donut-shaped.' My hair, being fed through the hole of the 'donut' was wrapped around it (the 'donut-ratt').

Sarah told me that you should rotate the 'ratt' as it was rolled down. That way it was easier to evenly distribute ('spread out' in her words) my hair around the 'ratt' ('ratt-donut,' in my words) completely covering and hiding it (the 'ratt-donut').

In my mind I pictured a rat holding a Cherrio in its paws. 'Cherrio' like the breakfast cereal. A 'rat donut.' Yeah, I'm the one who's 'dingue' (French for crazy). I admit it!

Finishing up, Sarah stuck in three (and only three) bobby pins to hold the bun in place. Well, almost finishing up. She then hairsprayed (Is that a word?) and combed the few disobedient (flyaway) hairs on my neck, around my ears and at my temples, 'gluing' them into place.

Amazingly, the entire process took less than thirty minutes. It would have taken much less time if Sarah hadn't insisted on getting every single hair in place! Also sparing me getting sprayed multiple times with shellac. (Oh, I know they don't use shellac anymore. It's been replaced with 'polymers,' according to Marty).

When the torture was over, I was actually quite happy with how I looked. I was going to have to get Sarah teach me how to do a French braid on myself. I might even try to see if Madame Roget would let me get away with wearing a braid during ballet class. (I doubt she would, though). A 'ratt-donut' bun would be a safer bet.

Anyway, we all ended up doing our own makeup. Emalie's was over-the-top in my opinion. Particularly her lipstick, it was bright red and very 1930s. Sarah's was absolutely natural looking. I watched her putting it on, so I knew she used a lot more than I did, but she didn't look like she had at all.

Me. I went with minimal: eyeliner, mascara and lip gloss. I was just going to go with just lip gloss, but to get Sarah and Emalie (especially) off my back, I gave in and used the eye stuff. Not eye shadow though. I mean I'm only a sixth grader!

The ball was okay. It would have been great if Marty had been there! But alas!

I group danced (danced with a group, but not with the same

steps at the same time). I only danced to up tempo music, though. Dancing solo to slow music is just too weird at a ball. Despite what Mme. Roget says.

Once I even did do a pirouette, which is difficult (for me) in heels. Especially three-inch ones. It would have definitely been much easier in chaussons!

I did it 'à la seconde' (with the working leg to the side), almost hitting a senior girl. Not a wise thing to do!

Later in the evening, there was this one 'local' (I had seen him around town) who sort of attached himself to our group (Emalie, me and various other first and second years). After he had been dancing with us (our group) for a while, a slow song came up and he asked me to dance with him.

I suspected that he had been thinking that he wasn't dancing with 'us,' but that he had been dancing with ME! It sort of freaked me out, but I was polite. I thanked him, but declined, saying I was tired.

I was a scaredy-cat! I could have told him, "Thanks, but I have a boyfriend." But no, I headed for the girls' bathroom. Then grabbed a cup of punch, found an empty table and sat out the next few songs (three to be exact!).

After a couple of songs, Emalie realized I was missing and searched and found me. She asked me what was wrong and I told her about the guy. Acting all nonchalant, she asked me which guy. I pointed him out and her immediate reaction was, "Wow! He's good looking!"

She droned on with, "From the way you were talking, I thought it was some loser. But that guy's really cute! Why didn't you dance with him?"

I responded that I had a boyfriend and wasn't interested in some guy I didn't even know holding me in a slow dance (which everyone else would be doing and not 'following the herd,' in Marty's words, would make everyone think I was weird). So there!

So, Emalie took another tack and tried to convince me, "Marty wouldn't mind you having fun by dancing with another guy. He's not the jealous type."

"Maybe… No, of course, he wouldn't mind. But I would! And as for 'fun,' it wouldn't be any!" I replied.

Of course, she wouldn't drop it there, so she went and found Sarah and dragged her over (which I'm sure neither she nor Aaron appreciated, as they were dancing a slow song!).

When Emalie explained why she had yanked her away from Aaron in the middle of a slow dance. Sarah snapped, "And for this, you pulled me away?" (from Aaron, of course!). Then she stomped back to him just as the song ended. Fortunately, though, another slow song followed that one.

Emalie just sat across the table from me and sulked silently, 'Dieu merci!' (Thank God!) and when the next song began (a fast tempo-ed one) she got up to go dance. When I didn't follow her lead (and remained seated), she growled, "Aren't you coming?"

When I replied (saccharinely sweet), "No, I think I'll sit out a few," she stomped off hunting for a group (or a guy if possible) to attach herself to.

Just to be cantankerous, I thought about sitting out a few more songs. But instead, I got up and danced, I started throwing in ballet moves (pirouettes, sautés, dégagés…). Everything but moves like glissés, fouettés or any échaînements that needed too much space (and posed the danger of colliding with other dancers, especially seniors!).

People started eyeing me. Some even stopped dancing and formed a sort of circle around me (which sort of weirded me out), but I was having fun.

As I kept on, two other ballerinas (of my year) joined me and we performed a choreography Mrs. Roget had been drilling into us. Then two advanced danseuses joined us and we ran though the routine again.

However, when those two went into another choreography, which we didn't know (and frankly, was way beyond our level of technique), the first years and I bowed out. To be honest, I was on my last legs (ha! ha!) and pooped out.

Emalie didn't come back until eleven, when the dance was over. It seems she did 'meet a boy!' (Sigh!). Sarah left with Aaron for their dessert and then they were driven home by Aaron's cousin, Isaac.

Written the week of the 17th to the 22nd of April, 1963.

Monday, April 22, 1963

Dr. Jameson,

I just reread this week's tome and realized that I've been writing a lot about clothes, hair, makeup and boys (well, Marty and the guy at the Winter Ball). Things I used to make fun of other girls going on and on about.

I don't think I'm boy-crazy like some of the girls in my classes, but I'm different from what I used to be. I mean until this last August, I always thought of Marty as just a friend.

But now I definitely think of him, as much more as you figured out at the Winter Ball this year. Though, at first, I wasn't happy with him when he gave me the 'kiddushin' ring!

As I've thought about it though, my objection is about how much he spent. I mean a ring worth over $3,000 is, well, just crazy. However, this is Marty and the social aspects of money isn't clear to him. He and I definitely have to talk about that.

I know you're concerned about the precocity (I think that's the right word) of our relationship, though Marty certainly has his foot on the brakes about that!

But other girls in first year with me talk about their boyfriends a lot. Mostly girls with boyfriends older than them by a couple of years to be truthful. But some admit (or claim) to be going a lot further than Marty and I have. I would feel weird talking about those kinds of things with anyone but my closest friends, like Sarah, or my sister, Karen. I wouldn't even talk to Mom, though there's not much she doesn't already know or strongly suspect.

What Marty and I have is really special, but I admit my emotions are confusing. I doubt there'll be time to discuss all this this week, but could we spend more time talking about it next week?

Croyez, Chère Docteur, à mes sentiments les meilleurs,
[Dear Doctor, my best wishes]

Jenny

P.S. That's hard to translate, but it's a polite greeting to a friend. If that's not being too impertinent on my part!

173

Journal: Monday, November, 26th to Friday, December, 15th, 1961

End of Term

The week after Thanksgiving, Mme. Roget told us she had heard about our "unauthorized performance" and also had heard that we made "many mistakes" in doing it. (I wondered who ratted us out. Probably some senior too chicken to join us!).

So, every day the next week, we spent ALL OF EVERY CLASS going through the choreography. Again and again and again. (Sigh! No good deed goes unpunished). And she had instructed us… In truth, she suggested (strongly, you might say) that we use some of our "movements de ballet" at the ball!

The next few of weeks went by in a blur, taken up as they were by writing term papers (for me, but not Sarah and Emalie) and exams for everyone.

Anyway, that fall's school semester did end up on a high note. Even though all my courses were above my grade level, I did get all A's (except for PE, like in the first grade).

Advanced Algebra wasn't all that enjoyable, but it went okay. The World Religions was really interesting and ended up being my favorite class. Psychology, even though it's a course for seniors, was really neat too. Biology was pretty boring. Too bad I couldn't have taken Human Anatomy like Marty did.

One thing I really did miss, though, was my swimming. There was just no swimming team anywhere nearby and it would have just been too hard to get to the Lynch/van Otterloo YMCA, where there was a team. To get there would have required three bus transfers. It would have taken forever!

So, Beginning Classical Dance (Ballet), like in the first grade, was the only class that first semester I didn't get an A in. A P.E. class, of course! (I got a B+). My first-grade experience all over again. (Sigh!).

As to problems that fall, it was Dad being at home that was hard. He usually went to his office at MIT during the day (even on Saturdays and Sundays), but on Thanksgiving, Christmas Eve and Christmas, he was at home the whole time. He told Karen that it "wouldn't look good" if he was in his office those days and not a home.

He did keep his word and left me alone, though. (Really, he avoided me like the plague!). I think Karen's threat to go to MIT's Dean of Faculty and/or the police put 'la peur de l'Éternel' (the fear of the LORD) in him.

One good thing concerning Dad was that he followed through on Karen's 'suggestion' that he go on (an early) sabbatical. At first, he planned be in Iran from August 15th, 1962 to January 15th, 1963. Studying the conflict between the Pahlavi Dynasty and the conservative Shiite clergy.

Then he got his sabbatical extended and would also be teaching seminars at the University of Tehran. That meant that he wouldn't be around at least from that next August until Easter break of 1963!

As you know, he got his time in Tehran extended, so he could continue his affair with his student as we found out this Thanksgiving.

Written the week of the 24th to the 29th of April, 1963.

Monday, April 29th, 1963

Dr. Jameson,

I have really come a long-ways in how I see that week in August of 1961. Writing about that Thursday that Dad emotionally abused (or molested) me has been difficult, but I now see his actions as mental abuse with sexual overtones. I think that is the case with Karen too. It could have easily turned into physical sexual abuse as I think it did with Mike, though.

All that has followed from that abuse has turned my family upside down, but your counsel has helped me deal with it. Not that I've somehow arrived at 'dénouement.' That's a French word that means 'untying.' Like in my literature class. It's means where the story ends and the main problems are resolved. A resolution of the questions raised.

Sorry, I'm sure you already know that. I can be as bad as Marty sometimes! What can you expect, I'm a nerd!

Anyway, I realize I'm not at 'resolution' yet and still need counseling. I hope your counseling. Even though I'm not in agreement with you on some things as my situation is different from most. (I guess you hear that often when your patients don't want to follow your recommendations or aren't ready to yet).

But I do listen to you and give what you say a lot of thought.

If it's okay with you, I'd like to change how we are doing my counseling a bit, though.

What started off as a diary journal of a week, turned into an account of the entire semester. I think I'd like to stop my missives with the end of the fall semester of 1961, though.

I think that last week's session where we ended up spending most of our time talking about Marty's and my relationship and what's going on in my life gave me a lot to consider. Not that I want to stop talking about the past, but I would like to have some help with things that are going on right now and might be happening in the future.

With Marty moving in with us next fall and my parent's divorce, a lot of adjustments will have to happen. I'll need your help with that and if I can keep seeing you that would be 'brilliant' as a Brit would say.]

Votre patiente dévouée,
Jenny

['Your devoted patient' is a more proper way to address oneself
to an esteemed psychologist and psychiatric mental health nurse
like yourself !]

Mon cher Marty,

Thank you for the beautiful roses! All the girls are really jealous and want a boyfriend like you! Don't let it go to your head, though. You're mine!

I just finished typing up the last page of my 'Journal' at noon yesterday, just in time for my session with Dr. Jameson today. I had agreed (sort of promised) to give my missives (as I call them) to the secretary before classes on Tuesday mornings, so Dr. Jameson could read them before our session.

However, I had a first draft of a term paper to turn in for World Religions and worked all night finishing it. We have to follow Kate Turabian's 'Manual for Writers of Term Papers, Theses and Dissertations' (which I'm sure you use with your students).

We had to use at least fifteen different sources and correctly (and exactly) follow Turabian's style manual for all the footnotes. Well, really, for everything.

I kept misjudging the space I needed at the bottom of the page for my citations and so had to keep retyping pages. How do YOU predict how much space you'll need?

I finally tried estimating the space by typing in my footnotes first and then typed the 'body' as Dr. Fields calls it. That helped, but sometimes I put in footnotes with text that I couldn't fit in and so the footnote didn't correspond to the text in 'pagination,' again as Dr. Fields calls it. I'm not talking about the allowed spillage of a text note to the next page (of which I had four).

Once I had too MUCH space for the 'body' left and then couldn't type in the first line of the next page because it had a footnote! I did a lot of retyping. Maybe you can help me when you come to Harvard next fall! (SMILE!).

When I finish this, I'm heading for the library to photocopy the last chapter of my journal, so I can send you your copy. I'm glad you got your student (or more properly 'tutee!'), Randy, to agree to let me send the journal to you through him. I certainly wouldn't have wanted Aunt May to get her hands on it!

When I started this counseling 'homework' for Dr. Jameson, I didn't realize how long it would be (the journal, I mean). But it has helped me get a 'clearer head' as opposed to a 'fuzzy' one. (I mean 'fuzzy' as in 'fuzzy thinking, so don't laugh!).

How have Uncle Roy and Aunt May reacted to the idea of me coming for the whole week for the reunion? Dad is such a sous-merde (below crappy!). I wasn't aware that he had been contributing anything, but to refuse to keep on doing it is 'dégueulasse' (despicable!). Why am I not surprised, though?

Well, I have to run if I'm going to get my stuff photocopied before the library closes. It's already fifteen 'til nine.

Thank you again for the beautiful roses. We're going to celebrate my birthday next Friday after classes at 'The Barnacle,' so today would have dreary without your thoughtfulness!

Je t'aime, Mon Cher Bien-Aimé,
Jenny

ABOUT THE AUTHOR

I'm Mary Jean White, a storyteller from a family of storytellers. At family reunions, instead of playing with my cousins, I hid in corners trying to remain unnoticed and listened. I eavesdropped on the grownups as they sat around dining room tables drinking iced tea and recounted happenings of the distant and not so distant past. Tales about family, friends and enemies filled those hot, humid, Southern afternoons of my childhood.

I grew up in the Tennessee River Valley. My family had been here since 1809, when John White, a scoundrel of an ancestor from Scotland, grabbed some land in Cherokee Territory. He kept from getting killed when skirmishes broke out between the white settlers and the Cherokees by marrying a Cherokee woman (and being adopted by her family, according to my Grandfather White's account).

Now I'm a retired professor of cultural anthropology. I speak seven languages and read an additional ten (some of which are dead languages only known through ancient documents). In my undergraduate studies, my academic advisor for my Senior Thesis was Joseph Campbell, the renowned mythologist. For my Phil.D., I read Comparative Religions and have done research in comparative mythology in the Americas, Europe, Africa and Oceania.

The one thing I really love is telling stories. Stories built on the myths of our beliefs. Myths of our families. Myths of our land. The myths of our truth. Myths that reflect our lives and who we are.

ABOUT THE EDITOR

I'm Mark White, a retired professor of Ethnomusicology. I was hesitant when my cousin, Mary Jean, came to me and asked me to edit her books. I was aware of her language proclivities all too well. As she would toss in words from French or German if, to quote her, "They fit the exact meaning I wanted better!" This, of course, left everyone scratching their heads and whispering to each other, "What did Mary Jean just say?"

I speak French, German, Portuguese, Spanish and Italian as well as English, which helps. As for the Old Norse, Icelandic, Old Babylonian, Hebrew, Aramaic, Ladino, Yiddish and, oh yes, Scots, Scottish Gaelic and Irish, Mary has tossed into her books, I won't even try. (My attitude is trust her or look it up yourself!).

As for editing (in English and French), I have forty years of experience serving on thesis and dissertation committees. After my retirement, I have worked as a consultant to students working on their dissertations.

This is my first time editing a work of popular fiction. I hope I've done a decent job of editing while remaining true to the stories and styles that could only have come my favorite *storyteller*, which according to Mary Jean, is *tusitala* in the Samoan language.

A note about the translations: Mary Jean didn't translate the Scots and Irish in her first manuscript. So, I had to get her to add those translations in, placing them in parentheses. I did the same for the French texts, which I translated. Of course, I had her read my translations to approve them, which she did for most part. I adopted hers, though, when she didn't think mine were the best.

Appalachian Publishing House

First Edition © 2019

Second Edition © 2020

All rights are reserved. This work is the property of the author, and the author retains full copyright in relation to printed material, whether on paper, digital or electronic media. No part of this publication may be reproduced, stored in a retrieval system, or transmitted in any form or by any means without the prior written permission of the author or unless paid for through sales channels authorized and approved by the author. The only exception are brief quotations in printed reviews.

For more information contact:

Appalachian Publishing House
P.O. Box 3664
Running Springs, California
92382-3664

www.ingramcontent.com/pod-product-compliance
Lightning Source LLC
Chambersburg PA
CBHW072010170726
47999CB00014B/1507